O. HENRY'S SHORT STORIES represent the
best work of the most popular master in this field.
Nearly every other writer who has made his mark
with the short story has also written novels; not so
with O. Henry. His reputation stands upon his
short stories alone. O. Henry was the *nom de
plume* of William Sydney Porter, who was born in
Greensboro, N. C., in 1862 and died in New York
in 1910. He lived for some years in Texas, wandered around Central America, and settled in New
York, which was always a city of wonder and
romance to him, "Bagdad-on-the-Subway." Critic
William Lyon Phelps said, "No writer of distinc-
tion has, I think, been more closely identified with
the short story in English than O. Henry."

**PUT PLEASURE IN YOUR READING
Larger type makes the difference
This EASY EYE Edition is set in large,
clear type—at least 30 percent larger
than usual. It is printed on non-glare
paper for better contrast and less eye-
strain.**

O. HENRY'S SHORT STORIES

MAGNUM EASY EYE BOOKS
MAGNUM BOOKS • NEW YORK

A MAGNUM EASY EYE BOOK

O. HENRY'S SHORT STORIES

THE RANSOM OF RED CHIEF copyright © 1907 by Doubleday
& Company, Inc., from WHIRLIGIGS; THE HALBERDIER OF
THE LITTLE RHEINSCHLOSS copyright © 1907 by Doubleday
& Company, Inc., from ROADS OF DESTINY; reprinted by per-
mission.

Special contents of this edition
copyright © 1968 by Lancer Books, Inc.
All rights reserved
Printed in the U.S.A.

PRESTIGE BOOKS INC. • 18 EAST 41ST STREET
NEW YORK, N.Y. 10017

Contents

5

THE LAST LEAF

IN A LITTLE DISTRICT west of Washington Square the streets have run crazy and broken themselves into small strips called "places." These "places" make strangle angles and curves. One street crosses itself a time or two. An artist once dicovered a valuable possibility in this street. Suppose a collector with a bill for paints, paper and canvas should, in traversing this route, suddenly meet himself coming back, without a cent having been paid on account!

So, to quaint old Greenwich Village the art people soon came prowling, hunting for north windows and eighteenth-century gables and Dutch attics and low rents. Then they imported some pewter mugs and a chafing dish or two from Sixth Avenue, and became a "colony."

At the top of a squatty, three-story brick Sue and Johnsy had their studio. "Johnsy" was familiar for Joanna. One was from Maine; the other from California. They had met at the *table d'hôte* of an Eighth Street "Delmonico's," and found their tastes in art, chicory salad and bishop sleeves so congenial that the joint studio resulted.

That was in May. In November a cold, unseen stranger, whom the doctors called Pneumonia, stalked about the colony, touching one here and there with his icy fingers. Over on the east side this ravager strode boldly, smiting his victims by scores, but his feet trod slowly through the maze of the narrow and moss-grown "places."

Mr. Pneumonia was not what you would call a chivalric old gentleman. A mite of a little woman with blood thinned by California zephyrs was hardly fair game for the red-fisted, short-breathed old duffer. But Johnsy he smote; and she lay, scarcely moving, on her painted iron bedstead, looking through the small Dutch window-panes at the blank side of the next brick house.

One morning the busy doctor invited Sue into the hallway with a shaggy, gray eyebrow.

"She has one chance in—let us say, ten," he said, as he shook down the mercury in his clinical thermometer. "And that chance is for her to want to live. This way people have of lining-up on the side of the undertaker makes the entire pharmacopoeia look silly. Your little lady has made up her mind that she's not going to get well. Has she anything on her mind?"

"She—she wanted to paint the Bay of Naples some day," said Sue.

"Paint?—bosh? Has she anything on her mind worth thinking about twice—a man, for instance?"

"A man?" said Sue, with a jew's-harp twang in her voice. "Is a man worth—but, no, doctor; there is nothing of the kind."

"Well, it is the weakness, then," said the doctor. "I will do all that science, so far as it may filter through my efforts, can accomplish. But whenever my patient begins to count the carriages in her funeral procession I subtract 50 per cent. from the curative power of medicines. If you will get her to ask one question about the new winter styles in cloak sleeves I will promise you a one-in-five chance for her, instead of one in ten."

After the doctor had gone Sue went into the workroom and cried a Japanese napkin to a pulp. Then she swaggered into Johnsy's room with her drawing board, whistling ragtime.

Johnsy, lay, scarcely making a ripple under the bedclothes, with her face toward the window. Sue stopped whistling, thinking she was asleep.

She arranged her board and began a pen-and-ink

drawing to illustrate a magazine story. Young artists must pave their way to Art by drawing pictures for magazine stories that young authors write to pave their way to Literature.

As Sue was sketching a pair of elegant horseshow riding trousers and a monocle on the figure of the hero, an Idaho cowboy, she heard a low sound, several times repeated. She went quickly to the bedside.

Johnsy's eyes were open wide. She was looking out the window and counting—counting backward.

"Twelve," she said, and a little later "eleven"; and then "ten," and "nine"; and then "eight" and "seven," almost together.

She looked solicitously out of the window. What was there to count? There was only a bare, dreary yard to be seen, and the blank side of the brick house twenty feet away. An old, old, ivy vine, gnarled and decayed at the roots, climbed half way up the brick wall. The could breath of autumn had stricken its leaves from the vine until its skeleton branches clung, almost bare, to the crumbling bricks.

"What is it, dear?" asked Sue.

"Six," said Johnsy, in almost a whisper. "They're falling faster now. Three days ago there were almost a hundred. It made my head ache to count them. But now its easy. There goes another one. There are only five left now."

"Five what, dear. Tell your Sudie."

"Leaves. On the ivy vine. When the last one falls I must go, too. I've known that for three days. Didn't the doctor tell you?"

"Oh, I never heard of such nonsense," complained Sue, with magnificent scorn. "What have old ivy leaves to do with your getting well? And you used to love that vine, so, you naughty girl. Don't be a goosey. Why, the doctor told me this morning that your chances for getting well real soon were—let's see exactly what he said—he said the chances were ten to one! Why, that's almost as good a chance as we have in New York when we ride on the street cars or walk past a new building. Try to take some broth now, and let Sudie go back to her drawing, so she can sell the editor man with it, and buy port wine for her sick child, and pork chops for her greedy self."

"You needn't get any more wine," said Johnsy, keeping her eyes fixed out the window. "There goes another. No, I don't want any broth. That leaves just four. I want to see the last one fall before it gets dark. Then I'll go, too."

"Johnsy, dear," said Sue, bending over her, "will you promise me to keep your eyes closed, and not look out the window until I am done working? I must hand those drawings in by to-morrow. I need the light, or I would draw the shade soon."

"Couldn't you draw in the other room?" asked Johnsy, coldly.

"I'd rather be here by you," said Sue. "Besides, I don't want you to keep looking at those silly ivy leaves."

"Tell me as soon as you have finished," said Johnsy, closing her eyes, and lying white and still as a fallen statue, "because I want to see the last one fall. I'm tired of waiting. I'm tired of thinking. I went to turn loose my hold on everything, and go sailing down, down, just like one of those poor, tired leaves."

"Try to sleep," said Sue. "I must call Behrman up to be my model for the old hermit miner. I'll not be gone a minute. Don't try to move 'til I come back."

Old Behrman was a painter who lived on the ground floor beneath them. He was past sixty and had a Michael Angelo's Moses beard curling down from the head of a satyr along the body of an imp. Behrman was a failure in art. Forty years he had wielded the brush without getting near enough to touch the hem of his Mistress's robe. He had been always about to paint a masterpiece, but had never yet begun it. For several years he had painted nothing except now and then a daub in the line of commerce or advertising. He earned a little by serving as a model to those young artists in the colony who could not pay the price of a professional. He drank gin to excess, and still talked of his coming masterpiece. For the rest he was a fierce little old man, who scoffed terribly at softness in any one, and who regarded himself as especial mastiff-in-waiting to protect the two young artists in the studio above.

Sue found Behrman smelling strongly of juniper berries in his dimly lighted den below. In one corner was a blank canvas on an easel that had been waiting there for twenty-five years to receive the first line of the masterpiece. She told him of Johnsy's fancy, and how she feared she would, indeed, light and fragile as a leaf herself, float away, when her slight hold upon the world grew weaker.

Old Behrman, with his red eyes plainly streaming shouted his contempt and derision for such idiotic imaginings.

"Vass!" he cried. "Is dere people in de world mit der foolishness to die because leafs dey drop off from a confounded vine? I haf not heard of such a thing. No, I will not bose as a model for your

13

fool hermit-dunderhead. Vy do you allow dot silly pusiness to come in der prain of her? Ach, dot poor leetle Miss Yohnsy."

"She is very ill and weak," said Sue, "and the fever has left her mind morbid and full of strange fancies. Very well, Mr. Behrman, if you do not care to pose for me, you needn't. But I think you are a horrid old—old flibbertigibbet."

"You are just like a woman!" yelled Behrman. "Who said I will not bose? Go on. I come mit you. For half an hour I haf peen trying to say dot I am ready to bose. Gott! dis is not any blace in which one so goot as Miss Johnsy shall lie sick. Some day I vill baint a masterpiece, and ve shall all go away. Gott! yes."

Johnsy was sleeping when they went upstairs. Sue pulled the shade down to the window-sill, and motion Behrman into the other room. In there they peered out the window fearfully at the ivy vine. Then they looked at each other for a moment without speaking. A persistent, cold rain was falling, mingled with snow. Behrman, in his old blue shirt, took his seat as the hermit-miner on an upturned kettle for a rock.

When Sue awoke from an hour's sleep the next morning she found Johnsy with dull, wide-open eyes staring at the drawn green shade.

14

"Pull it up; I want to see," she ordered, in a whisper.

Wearily Sue obeyed.

But, lo! after the beating rain and fierce gusts of wind that had endured through the livelong night, there yet stood out against the brick wall one ivy leaf. It was the last one on the vine. Still dark green near its stem, but with its serrated edges tinted with the yellow of dissolution and decay, it hung bravely from a branch some twenty feet above the ground.

"It is the last one," said Johnsy. "I thought it would surely fall during the night. I heard the wind. It will fall to-day, and I shall die at the same time."

"Dear, dear!" said Sue, leaning her worn face down to the pillow, "think of me, if you won't think of yourself? What would I do?"

But Johnsy did not answer. The lonesomest thing in all the world is a soul when it is making ready to go on its mysterious, far journey. The fancy seemed to possess her more strongly as one by one the ties that bound her to friendship and to earth were loosed.

The day wore away, and even through the twilight they could see the lone ivy leaf clinging to its stem against the wall. And then, with the coming of the night the north wind was again loosed, while the rain still beat against the windows and pattered down from the low Dutch eaves.

When it was light enough Johnsy, the merciless, commanded that the shade be raised.

The ivy leaf was still there.

Johnsy lay for a long time looking at it. And then she called to Sue, who was stirring her chicken broth over the gas stove.

"I've been a bad girl, Sudie," said Johnsy. "Something has made that last leaf stay there to show me how wicked I was. It is a sin to want to die. You may bring me a little broth now, and some milk with a little port in it, and—no; bring me a hand-mirror first, and then pack some pillows about me, and I will sit up and watch you cook."

An hour later she said.

"Sudie, some day I hope to paint the Bay of Naples."

The doctor came in the afternoon, and Sue had an excuse to go into the hallway as he left.

"Even chances," said the doctor, taking Sue's thin, shaking hand in his. "With good nursing you'll win. And now I must see another case I have downstairs. Behrman, his name is—some kind of an artist, I believe. Pneumonia, too. He is an old, weak man, and the attack is acute. There is no hope for him; but he goes to the hospital to-day to be made more comfortable."

The next day the doctor said to Sue: "She's out of danger. You've won. Nutrition and care now—that's all."

And that afternoon Sue came to the bed where Johnsy lay, contentedly knitting a very blue and very useless woollen shoulder scarf, and put one arm around her, pillows and all.

"I have something to tell you, white mouse," she said. "Mr. Behrman died of pneumonia to-day in the hospital. He was ill only two days. The janitor found him on the morning of the first day in his room downstairs helpless with pain. His shoes and clothing were wet through and icy cold. They couldn't imagine where he had been on such a dreadful night. And then they found a lantern, still lighted, and a ladder that had been dragged from its place, and some scattered brushes, and a palette with green and yellow colors mixed on it, and—look out the window, dear, at the last ivy leaf on the wall. Didn't you wonder why it never fluttered or moved when the wind blew? Ah, darling, it's Behrman's masterpiece—he painted it there the night that the last leaf fell."

THE GIFT OF THE MAGI

ONE DOLLAR and eighty-seven cents. That was all. And sixty cents of it was in pennies. Pennies saved one and two at a time by bulldozing the grocer and the vegetable man and the butcher until one's cheeks burned with the silent imputation of parsimony that such close dealing implied. Three times Della counted it. One dollar and eighty-seven cents. And the next day would be Christmas.

There was clearly nothing to do but flop down on the shabby little couch and howl. So Della did it. Which instigates the moral reflection that life is made up of sobs, sniffles, and smiles, with sniffles predominating.

While the mistress of the home is gradually subsiding from the first stage to the second, take a look at the home. A furnished flat at $8 per week. It did not exactly beggar description, but it certainly had that word on the lookout for the mendicancy squad.

In the vestibule below was a letter-box into which no letter would go, and an electric button from which no mortal finger could coax a ring. Also appertaining thereunto was a card bearing the name "Mr. James Dillingham Young."

The "Dillingham" had been flung to the breeze during a former period of prosperity when its possessor was being paid $30 per week. Now, when the income was shrunk to $20, the letters of "Dillingham" looked blurred, as though they were thinking seriously of contracting to a modest and unassuming D. But whenever Mr. James Dillingham Young came home and reached his flat above he was called "Jim" and greatly hugged by Mrs. James Dillingham Young, already introduced to you as Della. Which is all very good.

Della finished her cry and attended to her cheeks with the powder rag. She stood by the window and looked out dully at a gray cat walking a gray fence in a gray backyard. Tomorrow would be Christmas Day, and she had only $1.87 with which to buy Jim a present. She had been saving every penny she could for months, with this result. Twenty dollars a week doesn't go far. Expenses had been greater than she had calculated. They always are. Only $1.87 to buy a present for Jim. Her Jim.

Many a happy hour she had spent planning for something nice for him. Something fine and rare and sterling—something just a little bit near to being worthy of the honor of being owned by Jim.

There was a pier-glass between the windows of the room. Perhaps you have seen a pier-glass in an $8 flat. A very thin and very agile person may, by observing his reflection in a rapid sequence of longitudinal strips, obtain a fairly accurate conception of his looks. Della, being slender, had mastered the art.

Suddenly, she whirled from the window and stood before the glass. Her eyes were shining brilliantly, but her face had lost its color within twenty seconds. Rapidly she pulled down her hair and let it fall to its full length.

Now, there were two possessions of the James Dillingham Youngs in which they both took a mighty pride. One was Jim's gold watch that had been his father's and his grandfather's. The other was Della's hair. Had the Queen of Sheba lived in the flat across the airshaft, Della would have let her hair hang out the window some day to dry just to depreciate Her Majesty's jewels and gifts. Had King Solomon been the janitor, with all his treasures piled up in the basement, Jim would have pulled out his watch every time he passed, just to see him pluck at his beard from envy.

So now Della's beautiful hair fell about her rippling and shining like a cascade of brown waters. It reached below her knee and made itself almost a garment for her. And then she did it up again nervously and quickly. Once she faltered for a minute and stood still while a tear or two splashed on the worn red carpet.

On went her old brown jacket; on went her old brown hat. With a whirl of skirts and with the brilliant sparkle still in her eyes, she fluttered out the door and down the stairs to the street.

Where she stopped the sign read: "Mme. Sofronie. Hair Goods of All Kinds." One flight up Della ran, and collected herself, panting. Madame, large, too white, chilly, hardly looked the "Sofronie."

"Will you buy my hair?" asked Della.

"I buy hair," said Madame. "Take yer hat off and let's have a sight at the looks of it."

Down rippled the brown cascade.

"Twenty dollars," said Madame, lifting the mass with a practised hand.

"Give it to me quick," said Della.

Oh, and the next two hours tripped by on rosy

wings. Forget the hashed metaphor. She was ransacking the stores for Jim's present.

She found it at last. It surely had been made for Jim and no one else. There was no other like it in any of the stores, and she had turned all of them inside out. It was a platinum fob chain simple and chaste in design, properly proclaiming its value by substance alone and not by meretricious ornamentation—as all good things should do. It was even worthy of The Watch. A soon as she saw it she knew that it must be Jim's. It was like him. Quietness and value—the description applied to both. Twenty-one dollars they took from her for it, and she hurried home with the 87 cents. With that chain on his watch Jim might be properly anxious about the time in any company. Grand as the watch was, he sometimes looked at it on the sly on account of the old leather strap that he used in place of a chain.

When Della reached home her intoxication gave way a little to prudence and reason. She got out her curling irons and lighted the gas and went to work repairing the ravages made by generosity added to love. Which is always a tremendous task, dear friends—a mammoth task.

Within forty minutes her head was covered with tiny, close-lying curls that made her look wonderfully like a truant schoolboy. She looked at her reflection in the mirror long, carefully, and critically.

"If Jim doesn't kill me," she said to herself, "before he takes a second look at me, he'll say I look like a Coney Island chorus girl. But what could I do—oh! what could I do with a dollar and eighty-seven cents?"

At 7 o'clock the coffee was made and the frying-pan was on the back of the stove hot and ready to cook the chops.

Jim was never late. Della doubled the fob chain in her hand and sat on the corner of the table near the door that he always entered. Then she heard his step on the stair away down on the first flight, and she turned white for just a moment. She had a habit of saying little silent prayers about the simplest everyday things, and now she whispered: "Please God, make him think I am still pretty."

The door opened and Jim stepped in and closed it. He looked thin and very serious. Poor fellow, he was only twenty-two—and to be burdened with a family! He needed a new overcoat and he was without gloves.

Jim stopped inside the door, as immovable as a setter at the scent of quail. His eyes were fixed upon Della, and there was an expression in them that she could not read, and it terrified her. It was not anger, nor surprise, nor disapproval, nor horror, nor any of the sentiments that she had been prepared for. He simply stared at her fixedly with that peculiar expression on his face.

Della wriggled off the table and went for him.

"Jim, darling," she cried, "don't look at me that way. I had my hair cut off and sold it because I couldn't have lived through Christmas without giving you a present. It'll grow out again—you won't mind, will you? I just had to do it. My hair grows awfully fast. Say 'Merry Christmas!' Jim, and let's be happy. You don't know what a nice—what a beautiful, nice gift I've got for you."

"You've cut off your hair?" asked Jim, laboriously, as if he had not arrived at that patent fact yet even after the hardest mental labor.

"Cut it off and sold it," said Della. "Don't you like me just as well, anyhow? I'm me without my hair, ain't I?"

Jim looked about the room curiously.

"You say your hair is gone?" he said, with an air almost of idiocy.

"You needn't look for it," said Della. "It's sold, I tell you—sold and gone, too. It's Christmas Eve, boy. Be good to me, for it went for you. Maybe the hairs of my head were numbered," she went on with a sudden serious sweetness, "but nobody could ever count my love for you. Shall I put the chops on, Jim?"

Out of his trance Jim seemed quickly to wake. He enfolded his Della. For ten seconds let us regard with discreet scrutiny some inconsequential object in the other direction. Eight dollars a week or a million a year—what is the difference? A mathematician or a wit would give you the wrong answer. The magi brought valuable gifts, but that was not among them. This dark assertion will be illuminated later on.

Jim drew a package from his overcoat pocket and threw it upon the table.

"Don't make any mistake, Dell," he said, "about me. I don't think there's anything in the way of a haircut or a shave or a shampoo that could make me like my girl any less. But if you'll unwrap that package you may see why you had me going a while at first."

White fingers and nimble tore at the string and paper. And then an ecstatic scream of joy; and then, alas! a quick feminine change to hysterical tears and wails, necessitating the immediate employment of all the comforting powers of the lord of the flat.

For there lay The Combs—the set of combs, side

and back, that Della had worshipped for long in a Broadway window. Beautiful combs, pure tortoise shell, with jewelled rims—just the shade to wear in the beautiful vanished hair. They were expensive combs, she knew, and her heart had simply craved and yearned over them without the least hope of possession. And now, they were hers, but the tresses that should have adorned the coveted adornments were gone.

But she hugged them to her bosom, and at length she was able to look up with dim eyes and a smile and say: "My hair grows so fast, Jim!"

And then Della leaped up like a little singed cat and cried, "Oh, oh!"

Jim had not yet seen his beautiful present. She held it out to him eagerly upon her open palm. The dull precious metal seemed to flash with a reflection of her bright and ardent spirit.

"Isn't it a dandy, Jim? I hunted all over town to find it. You'll have to look at the time a hundred times a day now. Give me your watch. I want to see how it looks on it."

Instead of obeying, Jim tumbled down on the couch and put his hands under the back of his head and smiled.

"Dell," said he, "let's put our Christmas presents away and keep 'em a while. They're too nice to use just at present. I sold the watch to get the money to buy your combs. And now suppose you put the chops on."

The magi, as you know, were wise men—wonderfully wise men—who brought gifts to the Babe in the manger. They invented the art of giving Christmas presents. Being wise, their gifts were no doubt wise ones, possibly bearing the privilege of exchange in case of duplication. And here I have lamely related to you the uneventful chronicle of two foolish children in a flat who most unwisely sacrificed for each other the greatest treasures of their house. But in a last word to the wise of these days let it be said that of all who give gifts these two were the wisest. Of all who give and receive gifts, such as they are wisest. Everywhere they are wisest. They are the magi.

THE GREEN DOOR

Suppose you should be walking down Broadway after dinner, with ten minutes allotted to the consummation of your cigar while you are choosing between a diverting tragedy and something serious in the way of vaudeville. Suddenly a hand is laid upon your arm. You turn to look into the thrilling eyes of a beautiful woman, wonderful in diamonds and Russian sables. She thrusts hurriedly into your hand an extremely hot buttered roll, flashes out a tiny pair of scissors, snips off the second button of your overcoat, meaningly ejaculates the one word, "parallelogram!" and swiftly flies down a cross street, looking back fearfully over her shoulder.

That would be pure adventure. Would you accept it! Not you. You would flush with embarrassment; you would sheepishly drop the roll and continue down Broadway, fumbling feebly for the missing button. This you would do unless you are one of the blessed few in whom the pure spirit of adventure is not dead.

True adventurers have never been plentiful. They who are set down in print as such have been mostly business men with newly invented methods. They have been out after the things they wanted—golden fleeces, holy grails, lady loves, treasure, crowns and fame. The true adventurer goes forth aimless and uncalculating to meet and greet unknown fate. A fine example was the Prodigal Son—when he started back home.

Half-adventurers—brave and splendid figures—have been numerous. From the Crusades to the Palisades they have enriched the arts of history and fiction and the trade of historical fiction. But each of them had a prize to win, a goal to kick, an axe to grind, a race to run, a new thrust in tierce to deliver, a name to carve, a crow to pick—so they were not followers of true adventure.

In the big city the twin spirits Romance and Adventure are always abroad seeking worthy wooers. As we roam the streets they slyly peep at us and challenge us in twenty different guises. Without knowing why, we look up suddenly to see in a window a face that seems to belong to our gallery of intimate portraits; in a sleeping thoroughfare we hear a cry of agony and fear coming from an empty and shuttered house; instead of at our familiar curb a cab-driver deposits us before a strange door, which one, with a smile, opens for us and bids us enter; a slip of paper, written upon, flutters down to our feet from the high lattices of Chance; we exchange glances of instantaneous hate, affection, and fear with hurrying strangers in the passing crowds; a sudden souse of rain—and our umbrella may be sheltering the daughters of the Full Moon and first cousin of the Sidereal System; at every corner handkerchiefs drop, fingers beckon, eyes besiege, and the lost, the lonely, the rapturous, the mysterious, the perilous changing clues of adventure are slipped into our fingers. But few of us are willing to hold and follow them. We are grown stiff with the ramrod of convention down our backs. We pass on; and some day we come, at the end of a very dull life, to reflect that our romance has been a pallid thing of a marriage or two, a satin rosette kept in a safe-deposit drawer, and a lifelong feud with a steam radiator.

Rudolf Steiner was a true adventurer. Few were the evenings on which he did not go forth from his hall bedchamber in search of the unexpected and the egregious. The most interesting thing in life seemed to him to be what might lie just around the next corner. Sometimes his willingness to tempt fate led him into strange paths. Twice he had spent the night in a station-house; again and again he had found himself the dupe of ingenious and mercenary tricksters; his watch and money had been the price of one flattering allurement. But with undiminished ardor he picked up every glove cast before him into the merry list of adventure.

One evening Rudolf was strolling along a cross-town street in the older central part of the city. Two streams of people filled the side-walks—the home-hurrying, and that restless contingent that abandons home for the specious welcome of the thousand-candle-power *table d'hôte.*

The young adventurer was of pleasing presence, and moved serenely and watchfully. By daylight he was a salesman in a piano store. He wore his tie drawn through a topaz ring instead of fastened with a stick pin; and once he had written to the editor of a magazine that "Junie's Love Test," by Miss Libbey, had been the book that had most influenced his life.

During his walk a violent chattering of teeth in a glass case on the sidewalk seemed at first to draw his attention (with a qualm) to a restaurant before which it was set; but a second glance revealed the electric letters of a dentist's sign high above the next door. A giant Negro, fantastically dressed in a red embroidered coat, yellow trousers and a military cap, discreetly distributed cards to those of the passing crowd who consented to take them.

This mode of dentistic advertising was a common sight to Rudolf. Usually he passed the dispenser of the dentist's cards without reducing his store; but to-night the African slipped one into his hand so deftly that he retained it there smiling a little at the successful feat.

When he had travelled a few yards further he glanced at the card indifferently. Surprised, he turned it over and looked again with interest. One side of the card was blank; on the other was written in ink three words, "The Green Door." And then Rudolf saw, three steps in front of him, a man throw down the card the Negro had given him as he passed. Rudolf picked it up. It was printed with the dentist's name and address and the usual schedule of "plate work" and "bridge work" and "crowns," and specious promises of "painless" operations.

The adventurous piano salesman halted at the corner and considered. Then he crossed the street walked down a block, recrossed and joined the upward current of people again. Without seeming to notice the Negro as he passed the second time, he carelessly took the card that was handed him. Ten steps away he inspected it. In the same handwriting that appeared on the first card "The Green Door" was inscribed upon it. Three or four cards were tossed to the pavement by pedestrians both following and leading him. These fell blank side up. Rudolf turned them over. Every one bore the printed legend of the dental "parlors."

Rarely did the arch sprite Adventure need to beckon twice to Rudolf Steiner, his true follower. But twice it had been done, and the quest was on.

Rudolf walked slowly back to where the giant Negro stood by the case of rattling teeth. This time as he passed he received no card. In spite of his gaudy and ridiculous garb, the Ethiopian displayed a natural barbaric dignity as he stood, offering the cards suavely to some, allowing others to pass unmolested. Every half minute he chanted a harsh, unintelligible phrase akin to the jabber of car conductors and grand opera. And not only did he withhold a card this time but it seemed to Rudolf that he received from the shining and massive black countenance a look of cold, almost contemptuous disdain.

The look stung the adventurer. He read in it a silent accusation that he had been found wanting. Whatever the mysterious written words on the from the throng for their recipient; and now cards might mean, the black had selected him twice seemed to have condemned him as deficient in the wit and spirit to engage the enigma.

Standing aside from the rush, the young man made a rapid estimate of the building in which he conceived that his adventure must lie. Five stories high it rose. A small restaurant occupied the basement.

The first floor, now closed, seemed to house millinery or furs. The second floor, by the winking electric letters, was the dentist's. Above this a polyglot babel of signs struggled to indicate the abodes of palmists, dressmakers, musicians, and doctors. Still higher up draped curtains and milk bottles white on the window sills proclaimed the regions of domesticity.

After concluding his survey Rudolf walked briskly up the high flight of stone steps into the house. Up two flights of the carpeted stairway he continued; and at its top paused. The hallway there was dimly lighted by two pale jets of gas—one far to his right, the other nearer, to his left. He looked toward the nearer light and saw, within its wan halo, a green door. For one moment he hesitated; then he seemed to see the contumelious sneer of the African juggler of cards; and then he walked straight to the green door and knocked against it.

Moments like those that passed before his knock was answered measure the quick breath of true adventure. What might not be behind those green panels! Gamesters at play; cunning rogues baiting their traps with subtle skill; beauty in love with courage, and thus planning to be sought by it; danger, death, love, disappointment, ridicule—any of these might respond to that temerarious rap.

A faint rustle was heard inside, and the door opened. A girl not yet twenty stood there white-faced and tottering. She loosed the knob and swayed weakly, groping with one hand. Rudolf caught her and laid her on a faded couch that stood against the wall. He closed the door and took a swift glance around the room by the light of a flickering gas jet. Neat, but extreme poverty was the story that he read.

The girl lay still, as if in a faint. Rudolf looked around the room excitedly for a barrel. People must be rolled upon a barrel who—no, no; that was for drowned persons. He began to fan her with his hat. That was successful, for he struck her nose with the brim of his derby and she opened her eyes. And then the young man saw that hers, indeed, was the one missing face from his heart's gallery of intimate portraits. The frank, gray eyes, the little nose, turning pertly outward; the chestnut hair, curling like the tendrils of a pea vine, seemed the right end and reward of all his wonderful adventures. But the face was woefully thin and pale.

The girl looked at him calmly, and then smiled.

"Fainted, didn't I?" she asked, weakly. "Well, who wouldn't? You try going without anything to eat for three days and see!"

"Himmel!" exclaimed Rudolf, jumping up. "Wait till I come back."

He dashed out the green door and down the stairs. In twenty minutes he was back again kicking at the door with his toe for her to open it. With both arms he hugged an array of wares from the grocery and the restaurant. On the table he laid them—bread and butter, cold meats, cakes, pies, pickles, oysters, a roasted chicken, a bottle of milk and one of red-hot tea.

"This is ridiculous," said Rudolf, blusteringly, "to

go without eating. You must quit making election bets of this kind. Supper is ready." He helped her to a chair at the table and asked: "Is there a cup for the tea?" "On the shelf by the window," she answered. When he turned again with the cup he saw her, with eyes shining rapturously, beginning upon a huge Dill pickle that she had rooted out from the paper bags with a woman's unerring instinct. He took it from her, laughingly, and poured the cup full of milk. "Drink that first," he ordered, "and then you shall have some tea, and then a chicken wing. If you are very good you shall have a pickle to-morrow. And now, if you'll allow me to be your guest we'll have supper."

He drew up the other chair. The tea brightened the girl's eyes and brought back some of her color. She began to eat with a sort of dainty ferocity like some starved wild animal. She seemed to regard the young man's presence and the aid he had rendered her as a natural thing—not as though she undervalued the conventions; but as one whose great stress gave her the right to put aside the artificial for the human. But gradually, with the return of strength and comfort, came also a sense of the little conventions that belong; and she began to tell him her little story. It was one of a thousand such as the city yawns at every day—the shop girl's story of insufficient wages, further reduced by "fines" that go to swell the store's profits; of time lost through illness; and then of lost positions, lost hope, and—the knock of the adventurer upon the green door.

But to Rudolf the history sounded as big as the Iliad or the crisis in "Junie's Love Test."

"To think of you going through all that," he exclaimed.

"It was something fierce," said the girl, solemnly.

"And you have no relatives or friends in the city?"

"None whatever."

"I am all alone in the world, too," said Rudolf, after a pause.

"I am glad of that," said the girl, promptly; and somehow it pleased the young man to hear that she approved of his bereft condition.

Very suddenly her eyelids dropped and she sighed deeply.

"I'm awfully sleepy," she said, "and I feel so good."

Rudolf rose and took his hat.

"Then I'll say good-night. A long night's sleep will be fine for you."

38

He held out his hand, and she took it and said "good-night." But her eyes asked a question so eloquently, so frankly and pathetically that he answered it with words.

"Oh, I'm coming back to-morrow to see how you are getting along. You can't get rid of me so easily."

Then, at the door, as though the way of his coming had been so much less important than the fact that he had come, she asked: "How did you come to knock at my door?"

He looked at her for a moment, remembering the cards, and felt a sudden jealous pain. What if they had fallen into other hands as adventurous as his? Quickly he decided that she must never know the truth. He would never let her know that he was aware of the strange expedient to which she had been driven by her great distress.

"One of our piano tuners lives in this house," he said. "I knocked at your door by mistake."

The last thing he saw in the room before the green door closed was her smile.

At the head of the stairway he paused and looked curiously about him. And then he went along the hallway to its other end; and, coming back, ascended to the floor above and continued his puzzled explorations. Every door that he found in the house was painted green.

Wondering, he descended to the sidewalk. The fantastic African was still there. Rudolf confronted him with his two cards in his hand.

"Will you tell me why you gave me these cards and what they mean?" he asked.

In a broad, good-natured grin the Negro exhibited a splendid advertisement of his master's profession.

"Dar it is, boss," he said, pointing down the street. "But I 'spect you is a little late for de fust act."

Looking the way he pointed Rudolf saw above the entrance to a theatre the blazing electric sign of its new play, "The Green Door."

"I'm informed dat it's a fust-rate show, sah," said the Negro. "De agent what represents it pussented me with a dollar, sah, to distribute a few of his cards along with de doctah's. May I offer you one of de doctah's cards, suh?"

At the corner of the block in which he lived Rudolf stopped for a glass of beer and a cigar. When he had come out with his lighted weed he buttoned his coat, pushed back his hat and said, stoutly, to the lamp post on the corner:

"All the same, I believe it was the hand of Fate that doped out the way for me to find her."

Which conclusion, under the circumstances, certainly admits Rudolf Steiner to the ranks of the true followers of Romance and Adventure.

ROADS OF DESTINY

I go to seek on many roads
What is to be.
True heart and strong, with love to light—
Will they not bear me in the fight
To order, shun or wield or mould
My Destiny?
Unpublished Poems of David Mignot.

THE SONG was over. The words were David's; the air, one of the countryside. The company about the inn table applauded heartily, for the young poet paid for the wine. Only the notary, M. Papineau, shook his head a little at the lines, for he was a man of books, and he had not drunk with the rest.

David went out into the village street, where the night air drove the wine vapor from his head. And

42

then he remembered that he and Yvonne had quarreled that day, and that he had resolved to leave his home that night to seek fame and honor in the great world outside.

"When my poems are on every man's tongue," he told himself, in a fine exhilaration, "she will, perhaps, think of the hard words she spoke this day."

Except the roysterers in the tavern, the village folk were abed. David crept softly into his room in the shed of his father's cottage and made a bundle of his small store of clothing. With this upon a staff, he set his face outward upon the road that ran from Vernoy.

He passed his father's herd of sheep huddled in their nightly pen—the sheep he herded daily, leaving them to scatter while he wrote verses on scraps of paper. He saw a light yet shining in Yvonne's window, and a weakness shook his purpose of a sudden. Perhaps that light meant that she rued, sleepless, her anger, and that morning—— But, no! His decision was made. Vernoy was no place for him. Not one soul there could share his thoughts. Out along that road lay his fate and his future.

Three leagues across the dim, moonlit champaign ran the road, straight as a plowman's furrow. It

was believed in the village that the road ran to
Paris, at least; and this name the poet whispered
to himself as he walked. Never so far from Vernoy
had David travelled before.

The Left Branch

*Three leagues, then, the road ran, and turned
into a puzzle. It joined with another and a larger
road at right angles. David stood, uncertain, for a
while, and then took the road to the left.*

Upon this more important highway were, im-
printed in the dust, wheel tracks left by the recent
passage of some vehicle. Some half an hour later
these traces were verified by the sight of a ponderous carriage mired in a little brook at the bottom
of a steep hill. The driver and postilions were shout-
ing and tugging at the horses' bridles. On the road
at one side stood a huge, black-clothed man and a
slender lady wrapped in a long, light cloak.

David saw the lack of skill in the efforts of the
servants. He quietly assumed control of the work.
He directed the outriders to cease their clamor at
the horses and to exercise their strength upon the
wheels. The driver alone urged the animals with
his familiar voice; David himself heaved a power-
ful shoulder at the rear of the carriage, and with
one harmonious tug the great vehicle rolled up on

solid ground. The outriders climbed to their places.

David stood for a moment upon one foot. The huge gentleman waved a hand. "You will enter the carriage," he said, in a voice large, like himself, but smoothed by art and habit. Obedience belonged in the path of such a voice. Brief as was the young poet's hesitation, it was cut shorter still by a renewal of the command. David's foot went to the step. In the darkness he perceived dimly the form of the lady upon the rear seat. He was about to seat himself opposite, when the voice again swayed him to its will. "You will sit at the lady's side."

The gentleman swung his great weight to the forward seat. The carriage proceeded up the hill. The lady was shrunk, silent, into her corner. David could not estimate whether she was old or young, but a delicate, mild perfume from her clothes stirred his poet's fancy to the belief that there was loveliness beneath the mystery. Here was an adventure such as he had often imagined. But as yet he held no key to it, for no word was spoken while he sat with his impenetrable companions.

In an hour's time David perceived through the window that the vehicle traversed the street of some town. Then it stopped in front of a closed and darkened house, and a postilion alighted to hammer impatiently upon the door A latticed window above flew wide and a night-capped head popped out.

"Who are ye that disturb honest folk at this time of night? My house is closed. 'Tis too late for profitable travellers to be abroad. Cease knocking at my door, and be off."

"Open!" spluttered the postilion, loudly; "open for Monseigneur the Marquis de Beaupertuys."

"Ah!" cried the voice above. "Ten thousand pardons, my lord. I did not know—the hour is so late—at once shall the door be opened, and the house placed at my lord's disposal."

Inside was heard the clink of chain and bar, and the door was flung open. Shivering with chill and apprehension, the landlord of the Silver Flagon stood, half clad, candle in hand, upon the threshold.

David followed the marquis out of the carriage. "Assist the lady," he was ordered. The poet obeyed. He felt her small hand tremble as he guided her descent. "Into the house," was the next command.

The room was the long dining-hall of the tavern. A great oak table ran down its length. The huge gentleman seated himself in a chair at the nearer end. The lady sank into another against the wall, with an air of great weariness. David stood, considering how best he might now take his leave and continue upon his way.

"My lord," said the landlord, bowing to the floor, "h-had I ex-expected this honor, entertainment would have been ready. T-t-there is wine and cold fowl and m-m-maybe——"

"Candles," said the marquis, spreading the fingers of one plump white hand in a gesture he had.

"Y-yes, my lord." He fetched half a dozen candles, lighted them, and set them upon the table.

"If monsieur would, perhaps, deign to taste a certain Burgundy—there is a cask——"

"Candles," said monsieur, spreading his fingers.

"Assuredly—quickly—I fly, my lord."

A dozen more lighted candles shone in the hall. The great bulk of the marquis overflowed his chair. He was dressed in fine black from head to foot save for the snowy ruffles at his wrist and throat. Even the hilt and scabbard of his sword were black. His expression was one of sneering pride. The ends of an upturned moustache reached nearly to his mocking eyes.

The lady sat motionless, and now David perceived that she was young, and possessed of pathetic and appealing beauty. He was startled from the contemplation of her forlorn loveliness by the booming voice of the marquis.

"What is your name and pursuit?"

"David Mignot. I am a poet."

The moustache of the marquis curled nearer to his eyes.

"How do you live?"

"I am also a shepherd; I guarded my father's flock," David answered, with his head high, but a flush upon his cheek.

"Then listen, master shepherd and poet, to the fortune you have blundered upon to-night. This lady is my niece, Mademoiselle Lucie de Varennes. She is of noble descent and is possessed of ten thousand francs a year in her own right. As to her charms, you have but to observe for yourself. If the inventory pleases your shepherd's heart, she becomes your wife at a word. Do not interrupt me. To-night I conveyed her to the château of the Comte de Villemaur, to whom her hand had been promised. Guests were present; the priest was waiting; her marriage to one eligible in rank and fortune was ready to be accomplished. At the altar this demoiselle, so meek and dutiful, turned upon me like a leopardess, charged me with cruelty and crimes, and broke, before the gaping priest, the troth I had plighted for her. I swore there and then, by ten thousand devils, that she should marry the first man we met upon leaving the château, be he prince, charcoal-burner, or thief. You, Shepherd, are the first. Mademoiselle must be wed this night.

If not you, then another. You have ten minutes in which to make your decision. Do not vex me with words or questions. Ten minutes, shepherd; and they are speeding."

The marquis drummed loudly with his white fingers upon the table. He sank into a veiled attitude of waiting. It was as if some great house had shut its doors and windows against approach. David would have spoken, but the huge man's bearing stopped his tongue. Instead, he stood by the lady's chair and bowed.

"Mademoiselle," he said, and he marvelled to find his words flowing easily before so much elegance and beauty. "You have heard me say I was a shepherd. I have also had the fancy, at times, that I am a poet. If it be the test of a poet to adore and cherish the beautiful, that fancy is now strengthened. Can I serve you in any way, mademoiselle?"

The young woman looked up at him with eyes dry and mournful. His frank, glowing face, made serious by the gravity of the adventure, his strong, straight figure and the liquid sympathy in his blue eyes, perhaps, also, her imminent need of long-denied help and kindness, thawed her to sudden tears.

"Monsieur," she said, in low tones, "you look to be true and kind. He is my uncle, the brother of my

49

father, and my only relative. He loved my mother, and he hates me because I am like her. He has made my life one long terror. I am afraid of his very looks, and never before dared to disobey him. But to-night he would have married me to a man three times my age. You will forgive me for bringing this vexation upon you, monsieur. You will, of course, decline this mad act he tries to force upon you. But let me thank you for your generous words, at least. I have had none spoken to me in so long."

There was now something more than generosity in the poet's eyes. Poet he must have been, for Yvonne was frogotten; this fine, new loveliness held him with its freshness and grace. The subtle perfume from her filled him with strange emotions. His tender look fell warmly upon her. She leaned to it, thirstily.

"Ten minutes," said David, "is given me in which to do what I would devote years to achieve. I will not say I pity you, mademoiselle; it would not be true—I love you. I cannot ask love from you yet, but let me rescue you from this cruel man, and, in time, love may come. I think I have a future, I will not always be a shepherd. For the present I will trust your fate to me, mademoiselle?"

"Ah, you would sacrifice yourself from pity!"

"From love. The time is almost up, mademoiselle."

"You will regret it, and despise me."

"I will live only to make you happy, and myself worthy of you."

Her fine small hand crept into his from beneath her cloak.

"I will trust you," she breathed, "with my life. And—and love—may not be so far off as you think. Tell him. Once away from the power of his eyes I may forget."

David went and stood before the marquis. The black figure stirred, and the mocking eyes glanced at the great hall clock.

"Two minutes to spare. A shepherd requires eight minutes to decide whether he will accept a bride of beauty and income! Speak up, shepherd, do you consent to become mademoiselle's husband?"

"Mademoiselle," said David, standing proudly, "has done me the honor to yield to my request that she become my wife."

"Well said!" said the marquis. "You have yet the making of a courtier in you, master shepherd. Mademoiselle could have drawn a worse prize, after all. And now to be done with the affair as quick as the Church and the devil will allow!"

51

He struck the table soundly with his sword hilt. The landlord came, knee-shaking, bringing more candles in the hope of anticipating the great lord's whims. "Fetch a priest," said the marquis, "a priest; do you understand? In ten minutes have a priest here, or——"

The landlord dropped his candles and flew.

The priest came, heavy-eyed and ruffled. He made David Mignot and Lucie de Varennes man and wife, pocketed a gold piece that the marquis tossed him, and shuffled out again into the night.

"Wine," ordered the marquis, spreading his ominous fingers at the host.

"Fill glasses," he said, when it was brought. He stood up at the head of the table in the candlelight, a black mountain of venom and conceit, with something like the memory of an old love turned to poison in his eye, as it fell upon his niece.

"Monsieur Mignot," he said, raising his wine-glass, "drink after I say this to you: You have taken to be your wife one who will make your life a foul and wretched thing. The blood in her is an inheritance running black lies and red ruin. She will bring you shame and anxiety. The devil that descended to her is there in her eyes and skin and mouth that stoop even to beguile a peasant. There is your

52

promise, monsieur poet, for a happy life. Drink your wine. At last, mademoiselle, I am rid of you."

The marquis drank. A little grievous cry, as if from a sudden wound, came from the girl's lips. David, with his glass in his hand, stepped forward three paces and faced the marquis. There was little of a shepherd in his bearing.

"Just now," he said calmly, "you did me the honor to call me 'monsieur.' May I hope, therefore, that my marriage to mademoiselle has placed me somewhat nearer to you in—let us say, reflected rank—has given me the right to stand more as an equal to monseigneur in a certain little piece of business I have in my mind?"

"You may hope, shepherd," sneered the marquis.

"Then," said David, dashing his glass of wine into the contemptuous eyes that mocked him, "perhaps you will condescend to fight me."

The fury of the great lord outbroke in one sudden curse like a blast from a horn. He tore his sword from its black sheath; he called to the hovering landlord: "A sword there, for this lout!" He turned to the lady, with a laugh that chilled her heart, and said: "You put much labor upon me madame. It seems I must find you a husband and make you a widow in the same night."

53

"I know not sword-play," said David. He flushed to make the confession before his lady.

" 'I know not sword-play,' " mimicked the marquis. "Shall we fight like peasants with oaken cudgels? *Hola!* François, my pistols!"

A postilion brought two shining great pistols ornamented with carven silver from the carriage holsters. The marquis tossed one upon the table near David's hand. "To the other end of the table," he cried; "even a shepherd may pull a trigger. Few of them attain the honor to die by the weapon of a De Beaupertuys."

The shepherd and the marquis faced each other from the ends of the long table. The landlord, in an ague of terror, clutched the air and stammered: "M-M-Monseigneur, for the love of Christ! not in my house!—do not spill blood—it will ruin my custom——" The look of the marquis, threatening him, paralyzed his tongue.

"Coward," cried the lord of Beaupertuys, "cease chattering your teeth long enough to give the word for us, if you can."

Mine host's knees smote the floor. He was without a vocabulary. Even sounds were beyond him. Still, by gestures he seemed to beseech peace in the name of his house and custom.

"I will give the word," said the lady, in a clear voice. She went up to David and kissed him sweetly. Her eyes were sparkling bright, and color had come to her cheek. She stood against the wall, and the two men levelled their pistols for her count.

"*Un—deux—trois!*"

The two reports came so nearly together that the candles flickered but once. The marquis stood, smiling, the fingers of his left hand resting, outspread, upon the end of the table. David remained erect, and turned his head very slowly, searching for his wife with his eyes. Then, as a garment falls from where it is hung, he sank, crumpled, upon the floor.

With a little cry of terror and despair, the widowed maid ran and stopped above him. She found his wound, and then looked up with her old look of pale melancholy. "Through his heart," she whispered. "Oh, his heart!"

"Come," boomed the great voice of the marquis, "out with you to the carriage! Daybreak shall not find you on my hands. Wed you shall be again, and to a living husband, this night. The next we come upon, my lady, highwayman or peasant. If the road yields no other, then the churl that opens my gates. Out with you to the carriage!"

The marquis, implacable and huge, the lady wrapped again in the mystery of her cloak, the postilion bearing the weapons—all moved out to the waiting carriage. The sound of its ponderous wheels rolling away echoed through the slumbering village. In the hall of the Silver Flagon the distracted landlord wrung his hands above the slain poet's body, while the flames of the four and twenty candles danced and flickered on the table.

The Right Branch

Three leagues, then, the road ran, and turned into a puzzle. It joined with another and a larger road at right angles. David stood, uncertain, for a while, and then took the road to the right.

Whither it led he knew not, but he was resolved to leave Vernoy far behind that night. He travelled a league and then passed a large château which showed testimony of recent entertainment. Lights shone from every window; from the great stone gateway ran a tracery of wheel tracks drawn in the dust by the vehicles of the guests.

Three leagues farther and David was weary. He rested and slept for a while on a bed of pine boughs at the roadside. Then up and on again along the unknown way.

Thus for five days he travelled the great road,

sleeping upon Nature's balsamic beds or in peasants' ricks, eating of their black, hospitable bread, drinking from streams or the willing cup of the goatherd.

At length he crossed a great bridge and set his foot within the smiling city that has crushed or crowned more poets than all the rest of the world. His breath came quickly as Paris sang to him in a little undertone her vital chant of greeting—the hum of voice and foot and wheel.

High up under the eaves of an old house in the Rue Conti, David paid for lodging, and set himself, in a wooden chair, to his poems. The street, once sheltering citizens of import and consequence, was now given over to those who ever follow in the wake of decline.

The houses were tall and still possessed of a ruined dignity, but many of them were empty save for dust and the spider. By night there was the clash of steel and the cries of brawlers straying restlessly from inn to inn. Where once gentility abode was now but a rancid and rude incontinence. But here David found housing commensurate to his scant purse. Daylight and candlelight found him at pen and paper.

One afternoon he was returning from a foraging trip to the lower world, with bread and curds and a bottle of thin wine. Halfway up his dark stairway he met—or rather came upon, for she rested on the stair—a young woman of a beauty that should balk even the justice of a poet's imagination. A loose, dark cloak, flung open, showed a rich gown beneath. Her eyes changed swiftly with every little shade of thought. Within one moment they would be round and artless like a child's, and long and cozening like a gypsy's. One hand raised her gown, undraping a little shoe, high-heeled, with its ribbons dangling, untied. So heavenly she was, so unfitted to stoop, so qualified to charm and command! Perhaps she had seen David coming, and had waited for his help there.

Ah, would monsieur pardon that she occupied the stairway, but the shoe—the naughty shoe. Alas! it would not remain tied. Ah! if monsieur *would* be so gracious!

The poet's fingers trembled as he tied the contrary ribbons. Then he would have fled from the danger of her presence, but the eyes grew long and cozening, like a gypsy's, and held him. He leaned against the balustrade, clutching his bottle of sour wine.

"You have been so good," she said, smiling. "Does monsieur, perhaps, live in the house?"

"Yes, madame. I—I think so, madame."

58

"Perhaps in the third story, then?"

"No, madame; higher up."

The lady fluttered her fingers with the least possible gesture of impatience.

"Pardon. Certainly I am not discreet in asking. Monsieur will forgive me? It is surely not becoming that I should inquire where he lodges."

"Madame, do not say so. I live in the——"

"No, no, no; do not tell me. Now I see that I erred. But I cannot lose the interest I feel in this house and all that is in it. Once it was my home. Often I come here but to dream of those happy days again. Will you let that be my excuse?"

"Let me tell you, then, for you need no excuse," stammered the poet. "I live in the top floor—the small room where the stairs turn."

"In the front room?" asked the lady, turning her head sidewise.

"The rear, madame."

The lady sighed, as if with relief.

"I will detain you no longer, then, monsieur," she said, employing the round and artless eye. "Take good care of my house. Alas! only the memories of it are mine now. Adieu, and accept my thanks for your courtesy."

She was gone, leaving but a smile and a trace of sweet perfume. David climbed the stairs as one in slumber. But he awoke from it, and the smile and the perfume lingered with him and never afterward did either seem quite to leave him. This lady of whom he knew nothing drove him to lyrics of eyes, chansons of swiftly conceived love, odes to curling hair, and sonnets to slippers on slender feet.

Poet he must have been, for Yvonne was forgotten; this fine, new loveliness held him with its freshness and grace. The subtle perfume about her filled him with strange emotions.

On a certain night three persons were gathered about a table in a room on the third floor of the same house. Three chairs and the table and a lighted candle upon it was all the furniture. One of the persons was a huge man, dressed in black. His expression was one of sneering pride. The ends of his upturned moustache reached nearly to his mocking eyes. Another was a lady, young and beautiful, with eyes that could be round and artless, like a child's, or long and cozening, like a gypsy's, but were now keen and ambitious, like any other conspirator's. The third was a man of action, a combatant, a bold and impatient executive, breathing fire and steel. He was addressed by the others as Captain Desrolles.

This man struck the table with his fist, and said, with controlled violence:

"To-night. To-night as he goes to midnight mass. I am tired of the plotting that gets nowhere. I am sick of signals and ciphers and secret meetings and such *baragouin*. Let us be honest traitors. If France is to be rid of him, let us kill in the open, and not hunt with snares and traps. To-night, I say. I back my words. My hand will do the deed. To-night, as he goes to mass."

The lady turned upon him a cordial look. Woman, however wedded to plots, must ever thus bow to rash courage. The big man stroked his upturned moustache.

"Dear captain," he said, in a great voice, softened by habit, "this time I agree with you. Nothing is to be gained by waiting. Enough of the palace guards belong to us to make the endeavor a safe one."

"To-night," repeated Captain Desrolles, again striking the table. "You have heard me, marquis; my hand will do the deed."

"But now," said the huge man, softly, "comes a question. Word must be sent to our partisans in the palace, and a signal agreed upon. Our stanchest men must accompany the royal carriage. At this hour what messenger can penetrate so far as the south doorway? Ribout is stationed there; once a message is placed in his hands, all will go well."

"I will send the message," said the lady.

"You, countess?" said the marquis, raising his eyebrows. "Your devotion is great, we know, but——"

"Listen!" exclaimed the lady, rising and resting her hands upon the table; "in a garret of this house lives a youth from the provinces as guileless and tender as the lambs he tended there. I have met him twice or thrice upon the stairs. I questioned him, fearing that he might dwell too near the room in which we are accustomed to meet. He is mine, if I will. He writes poems in his garret, and I think he dreams of me. He will do what I say. He shall take the message to the palace."

The marquis rose from his chair and bowed. "You did not permit me to finish my sentence, countess," he said. "I would have said: 'Your devotion is great, but your wit and charm are infinitely greater.'"

While the conspirators were thus engaged, David was polishing some lines addressed to his *amorette d'escalier*. He heard a timorous knock at his door, and opened it, with a great throb, to behold her there, panting as one in straits, with eyes wide open and artless, like a child's.

"Monsieur," she breathed, "I come to you in distress. I believe you to be good and true, and I know of no other help. How I flew through the streets among the swaggering men! Monsieur, my mother is dying. My uncle is a captain of guards in the palace of the king. Some one must fly to bring him. May I hope——"

"Mademoiselle," interrupted David, his eyes shining with the desire to do her service, "your hopes shall be my wings. Tell me how I may reach him."

The lady thrust a sealed paper into his hand.

"Go to the south gate—the south gate, mind— and say to the guards there, 'The falcon has left his nest.' They will pass you, and you will go to the south entrance to the palace. Repeat the words, and give this letter to the man who will reply 'Let him strike when he will.' This is the password, mon- sieur, entrusted to me by my uncle, for now when the country is disturbed and men plot against the king's life, no one without it can gain entrance to the palace grounds after nightfall. If you will, monsieur, take him this letter so that my mother may see him before she closes her eyes."

"Give it me," said David, eagerly. "But shall I let you return home through the streets alone so late? I——"

"No, no—fly. Each moment is like a precious jewel. Some time," said the lady, with eyes long and cozéning, like a gypsy's, "I will try to thank you for your goodness."

The poet thrust the letter into his breast, and bounded down the stairway. The lady, when he was gone, returned to the room below.

The eloquent eyebrows of the marquis interrogated her.

"He is gone," she said, "as fleet and stupid as one of his own sheep, to deliver it."

The table shook again from the batter of Captain Derolles's fist.

"Sacred name!" he cried; "I have left my pistols behind! I can trust no others."

"Take this," said the marquis, drawing from beneath his cloak a shining, great weapon, ornamented with carven silver. "There are none truer. But guard it closely, for it bears my arms and crest, and already I am suspected. Me, I must put many leagues between myself and Paris this night. Tomorrow must find me in my château. After you, dear countess."

The marquis puffed out the candle. The lady, well cloaked, and the two gentlemen softly descended the stairway and flowed into the crowd that roamed along the narrow pavements of the Rue Conti.

David sped. At the south gate of the king's residence a halberd was laid to his breast, but he turned its point with the words: "The falcon has left his nest."

"Pass, brother," said the guard, "and go quickly."

On the south steps of the palace they moved to seize him, but again the *mot de passe* charmed the watchers. One among them stepped forward and began: "Let him strike——" But a flurry among the guards told of a surprise. A man of keen look and soldierly stride suddenly pressed through them and seized the letter which David held in his hand. "Come with me," he said, and led him inside the great hall. Then he tore open the letter and read it. He beckoned to a man uniformed as an officer of musketeers, who passing. "Captain Tetreau, you will have the guards at the south entrance and the south gate arrested and confined. Place men known to be loyal in their places." To David he said: "Come with me."

He conducted him through a corridor and an anteroom into a spacious chamber, where a melancholy man, sombrely dressed, sat brooding in a great leather-covered chair. To that man he said:

"Sire, I have told you that the palace is as full of traitors and spies as a sewer is of rats. You have thought, sire, that it was my fancy. This man penetrated to your very door by their connivance. He bore a letter which I have intercepted. I have brought him here that your majesty may no longer think my zeal excessive."

"I will question him," said the king, stirring in his chair. He looked at David with heavy eyes dulled by an opaque film. The poet bent his knee.

"From where do you come?" asked the king.

"From the village of Vernoy, in the province of Eure-et-Loir, sire."

"What do you follow in Paris?"

"I—I would be a poet, sire."

"What did you in Vernoy?"

"I minded my father's flock of sheep."

The king stirred again, and the film lifted from his eyes.

"Ah! in the fields?"

"Yes, sire."

"You lived in the fields; you went out in the cool of the morning and lay among the hedges in the grass. The flock distributed itself upon the hillside; you drank of the living stream; you ate your sweet brown bread in the shade; and you listened, doubt-

66

less, to blackirds piping in the grove. Is not that so, shepherd?"

"It is, sire," answered David, with a sigh; "and to the bees at the flowers, and, maybe, to the grape gatherers singing on the hill."

"Yes, yes," said the king, impatiently; "maybe to them; but surely to the blackbirds. They whistled often, in the grove, did they not?"

"Nowhere, sire, so sweetly as in the Eure-et-Loir. I have endeavored to express their song in some verses that I have written."

"Can you repeat those verses?" asked the king, eagerly. "A long time ago I listened to the blackbirds. It would be something better than a kingdom if one could rightly construe their song. And at night you drove the sheep to the fold and then sat, in peace and tranquility, to your pleasant bread. Can you repeat those verses, shepherd?"

"They run this way, sire," said David, with respectful ardor:

"Lazy shepherd, see your lambkins
    Skip, ecstatic, on the mead;

See the firs dance in the breezes,
    Hear Pan blowing at his reed.

67

"Hear us calling from the tree-tops,
　See us swoop upon your flock;
Yield us wool to make our nests warm
　In the branches of the——"

"If it please your majesty," interrupted a harsh voice, "I will ask a question or two of this rymester. There is little time to spare. I crave pardon, sire, if my anxiety for your safety offends.'

"The loyalty," said the king, "of the Duke d'Aumale is too well proven to give offence." He sank into his chair, and the film came again over his eyes.

"First," said the duke, "I will read you the letter he brought:

"To-night is the anniversary of the dauphin's death. If he goes, as is his custom, to midnight mass to pray for the soul of his son, the falcon will strike, at the corner of the Rue Esplanade. If this be his intention, set a red light in the upper room at the southwest corner of the palace, that the falcon may take heed.

"Peasant," said the duke, sternly, "you have heard these words. Who gave you this message to bring?'

"My lord duke," said David, sincerely, "I will tell you. A lady gave it me. She said her mother was ill, and that this writing would fetch her uncle to her bedside. I do not know the meaning of the letter, but I will swear that she is beautiful and good."

"Describe the woman," commanded the duke, "and how you came to be her dupe."

"Describe her!" said David with a tender smile. "You would command words to perform miracles. Well, she is made of sunshine and deep shade. She is slender, like the alders, and moves with their grace. Her eyes change while you gaze into them; now round, and then half shut as the sun peeps between two clouds. When she comes, heaven is all about her; when she leaves, there is chaos and a scent of hawthorn blossoms. She came to me in the Rue Conti, number twenty-nine."

"It is the house," said the duke, turning to the king, "that we have been watching. Thanks to the poet's tongue, we have a picture of the infamous Countess Quebedaux."

"Sire and my lord duke," said David, earnestly, "I hope my poor words have done no injustice. I have looked into that lady's eyes. I will stake my life that she is an angel, letter or no letter."

The duke looked at him steadily. "I will put you to the proof," he said slowly. "Dressed as the king, you shall, yourself, attend mass in his carriage at midnight. Do you accept the test?"

David smiled. "I have looked into her eyes," he said. "I had my proof there. Take yours how you will."

Half an hour before twelve the Duke d'Aumale, with his own hands, set a red lamp in a southwest window of the palace. At ten minutes to the hour, David, leaning on his arm, dressed as the king, from top to toe, with his head bowed in his cloak, walked slowly from the royal apartments to the waiting carriage. The duke assisted him inside and closed the door. The carriage whirled away along its route to the cathedral.

On the *qui vive* in a house at the corner of the Rue Esplanade was Captain Tretreau with twenty men, ready to pounce upon the conspirators when they should appear.

But it seemed that, for some reason, the plotters had slightly altered their plans. When the royal carriage had reached the Rue Christopher, one square nearer than the Rue Esplanade, forth from it burst Captain Desrolles, with his band of would-be regicides, and assailed the equipage. The guards upon the carriage, though surprised at the premature attack, descended and fought valiantly. The noise of conflict attracted the force of Captain Tetreau, and they came pelting down the street to the rescue. But, in the meantime, the desperate

Desrolles had torn open the door of the king's carriage, thrust his weapon against the body of the dark figure inside, and fired.

Now, with loyal reinforcements at hand, the street rang with cries and the rasp of steel, but the frightened horses had dashed away. Upon the cushions lay the dead body of the poor mock king and poet, slain by a ball from the pistol of Monseigneur, the Marquis de Beaupertuys.

The Main Road

Three leagues, then, the road ran, and turned into a puzzle. It joined with another and a larger road at right angles. David stood, uncertain, for a while, and then sat himself to rest upon its side.

Whither those roads led he knew not. Either way there seemed to lie a great world full of chance and peril. And then, sitting there, his eye fell upon a bright star, one that he and Yvonne had named for theirs. That set him thinking of Yvonne, and he wondered if he had not been too hasty. Why should he leave her and his home because a few hot words had come between them? Was love so brittle a thing that jealousy, the very proof of it, could break it? Mornings always brought a cure for the little heartaches of evening. There was yet time for him to return home without any one in the sweetly

71

sleeping village of Vernoy being the wiser. His heart was Yvonne's; there where he had lived always he could write his poems and find his happiness.

David rose, and shook off his unrest and the wild mood that had tempted him. He set his face steadfastly back along the road he had come. By the time he had retravelled the road to Vernoy, his desire to rove was gone. He passed the sheepfold, and the sheep scurried, with a drumming flutter, at his late footsteps, warming his heart by the homely sound. He crept without noise into his little room and lay there, thankful that his feet had escaped the distress of new roads that night.

How well he knew woman's heart! The next evening Yvonne was at the well in the road where the young congregated in order that the *curé* might have business. The corner of her eye was engaged in a search for David, albeit her set mouth seemed unrelenting. He saw the look; braved the mouth, drew from it a recantation and, later, a kiss as they walked homeward together.

Three months afterward they were married. David's father was shrewd and prosperous. He gave them a wedding that was heard of three leagues away. Both the young people were favorites in the village. There was a procession in the streets, a dance on the green; they had the marionettes and a tumbler out from Dreux to delight the guests.

Then a year, and David's father died. The sheep and the cottage descended to him. He already had the seemliest wife in the village. Yvonne's milk pails and her brass kettles were bright—*ouf!* they blinded you in the sun when you passed that way. But you must keep your eyes upon her yard, for her flower beds were so neat and gay they restored to you your sight. And you might hear her sing, aye, as far as the double chestnut tree above Père Gruneau's blacksmith forge.

But a day came when David drew out paper from a long-shut drawer, and began to bite the end of a pencil. Spring had come again and touched his heart. Poet he must have been, for now Yvonne was well-nigh forgotten. This fine new loveliness of earth held him with its witchery and grace. The perfume from her woods and meadows stirred him strangely. Daily had he gone forth with his flock, and brought it safe at night. But now he stretched himself under the hedge and pieced words together on his bits of paper. The sheep strayed, and the wolves, perceiving that difficult poems make easy mutton, ventured from the woods and stole his lambs.

73

David's stock of poems grew larger and his flock smaller. Yvonne's nose and temper waxed sharp and her talk blunt. Her pans and kettles grew dull, but her eyes had caught their flash. She pointed out to the poet that his neglect was reducing the flock and bringing woe upon the household. David hired a boy to guard the sheep, locked himself in the little room in the top of the cottage, and wrote more poems. The boy, being a poet by nature, but not furnished with an outlet in the way of writing, spent his time in slumber. The wolves lost no time in discovering that poetry and sleep are practically the same; so the flock steadily grew smaller. Yvonne's ill temper increased at an equal rate. Sometimes she would stand in the yard and rail at David through his high window. Then you could hear her as far as the double chestnut tree above Père Gruneau's blacksmith forge.

M. Papineau, the kind, wise, meddling old notary, saw this, as he saw everything at which his nose pointed. He went to David, fortified himself with a great pinch of snuff, and said:

"Friend Mignot, I affixed the seal upon the marriage certificate of your father. It would distress me to be obliged to attest a paper signifying the bankruptcy of his son. But that is what you are coming to. I speak as an old friend. Now, listen to what I have to say. You have your heart set, I perceive, upon poetry. At Dreux, I have a friend, one Monsieur Bril—Georges Bril. He lives in a little cleared space in a houseful of books. He is a learned man; he visits Paris each year; he himself has written books. He will tell you when the catacombs were made, how they found out the names of the stars, and why the plover has a long bill. The meaning and the form of poetry is to him as intelligent as the baa of a sheep is to you. I will give you a letter to him, and you shall take him your poems and let him read them. Then you will know if you shall write more, or give your attention to your wife and business."

"Write the letter," said David. "I am sorry you did not speak of this sooner."

At sunrise the next morning he was on the road to Dreux with the precious toll of poems under his arm. At noon he wiped the dust from his feet at the door of Monsieur Bril. That learned man broke the seal of M. Papineau's letter, and sucked up its contents through his gleaming spectacles as the sun draws water. He took David inside to his study and sat him down upon a little island beat upon by a sea of books.

Monsieur Bril had a conscience. He flinched not even at a mass of manuscript the thickness of a finger length and rolled to an incorrigible curve. He broke the back of the roll against his knee and began to read. He slighted nothing; he bored into the lump as a worm into a nut, seeking for a kernel.

Meanwhile, David sat, marooned, trembling in the spray of so much literature. It roared in his ears. He held no chart or compass for voyaging in that sea. Half the world, he thought, must be writing books.

Monsieur Bril bored to the last page of the poems. Then he took off his spectacles and wiped them with his handkerchief.

"My old friend, Papineau, is well?" he asked.

"In the best of health," said David.

"How many sheep have you, Monsieur Mignot?"

"Three hundred and nine, when I counted them yesterday. The flock had had ill fortune. To that number it has decreased from eight hundred and fifty."

"You have a wife and a home, and lived in comfort. The sheep brought you plenty. You went into the fields with them and lived in the keen air and ate the sweet bread of contentment. You had but to be vigilant and recline there upon nature's breast, listening to the whistle of the blackbirds in the grove. Am I right thus far?"

"It was so," said David.

"I have read all your verses," continued Monsieur Bril, his eyes wandering about his sea of books as if he conned the horizon for a sale. "Look yonder, through that window, Monsieur Mignot; tell me what you see in that tree."

"I see a crow," said David, looking.

"There is a bird," said Monsieur Bril, "that shall assist me where I am disposed to shirk a duty. You know that bird, Monsieur Mignot; he is the philosopher of the air. He is happy through submission to his lot. None so merry or full-crawed as he with his whimsical eye and rollicking step. The fields yield him what he desires. He never grieves that his plumage is not gay, like the oriole's. And you have heard, Monsieur Mignot, the notes that nature has given him? Is the nightingale any happier, do you think?"

David rose to his feet. The crow cawed harshly from his tree.

"I thank you, Monsieur Bril," he said, slowly. "There was not, then, one nightingale note among all those croaks?"

"I could not have missed it," said Monsieur Bril, with a sigh. "I read every word. Live your poetry, man; do not try to write it any more."

"I thank you," said David, again. "And now I will be going back to my sheep."

"If you would dine with me," said the man of books, "and overlook the smart of it, I will give you reasons at length."

"No," said the poet, "I must be back in the fields cawing at my sheep."

Back along the road to Vernoy he trudged with his poems under his arm. When he reached his village he turned into the shop of one Zeigler, a Jew out of Armenia, who sold anything that came to his hand.

"Friend," said David, "wolves from the forest harass my sheep on the hills. I must purchase firearms to protect them. What have you?"

"A bad day, this, for me, friend Mignot," said Zeigler, spreading his hands, "for I perceive that I must sell you a weapon that will not fetch a tenth of its value. Only last week I bought from a peddler a wagon full of goods that he procured at a sale by a *commissionaire* of the crown. The sale was of the château and belongings of a great lord—I know not his title—who has been banished for conspiracy against the king. There are some choice firearms in the lot. This pistol—oh, a weapon fit for a prince!—it shall be only forty francs to you, friend

Mignot—if I lost ten by the sale. But perhaps an arquebuse——"

"This will do," said David, throwing the money on the counter. "Is it charged?"

"I will charge it," said Zeigler. "And, for ten francs more, add a store of powder and ball."

David laid his pistol under his coat and walked to his cottage. Yvonne was not there. Of late she had taken to gadding much among the neighbors. But a fire was glowing in the kitchen stove. David opened the door of it and thrust his poems in upon the coals. As they blazed up they made a singing, harsh sound in the flue.

"The song of the crow!" said the poet.

He went up to his attic room and closed the door. So quiet was the village that a score of people heard the roar of the great pistol. They flocked thither, and up the stairs where the smoke, issuing, drew their notice.

The man laid the body of the poet upon his bed, awkwardly arranging it to conceal the torn plumage of the poor black crow. The women chattered in a luxury of zealous pity. Some of them ran to tell Yvonne.

M. Papineau, whose nose had brought him there among the first, picked up the weapon and ran his eye over its silver mountings with a mingled air of connoisseurship and grief.

"The arms," he explained, aside, to the *curé*, "and crest of Monseigneur, the Marquis de Beaupertuys."

THE RANSOM OF RED CHIEF

IT LOOKED like a good thing: but wait till I tell you. We were down South, in Alabama—Bill Driscoll and myself—when this kidnapping idea struck us. It was, as Bill afterward expressed it, "during a moment of temporary mental apparition"; but we didn't find that out till later.

There was a town down there, as flat as a flannel-cake, and called Summit, of course. It contained inhabitants of as undeleterious and self-satisfied a class of peasantry as ever clustered around a Maypole.

Bill and me had a joint capital of about six hundred dollars, and we needed just two thousand dollars more to pull off a fraudulent town-lot scheme in Western Illinois with. We talked it over on the front steps of the hotel. Philoprogenitiveness, says we, is strong in semi-rural communities; therefore, and for other reasons, a kidnapping project ought to do better there than in the radius of newspapers that send reporters out in plain clothes to stir up talk about such things. We knew that Summit couldn't get after us with anything stronger than constables and, maybe, some lackadaisical bloodhounds and a diatribe or two in the *Weekly Farmers' Budget*. So, it looked good.

We selected for our victim the only child of a prominent citizen named Ebenezer Dorset. The father was respectable and tight, a mortgage fancier and a stern, upright collection-plate passer and forecloser. The kid was a boy of ten, with bas-relief freckles, and hair the color of the cover of the magazine you buy at the news-stand when you want to catch a train. Bill and me figured that Ebenezer would melt down for a ransom of two thousand dollars to a cent. But wait till I tell you.

About two miles from Summit was a little mountain, covered with a dense cedar brake. On the rear elevation of this mountain was a cave. There we stored provisions.

One evening after sundown, we drove in a buggy past old Dorset's house. The kid was in the street, throwing rocks at a kitten on the opposite fence.

"Hey, little boy!" says Bill, "would you like to have a bag of candy and a nice ride?"

The boy catches Bill neatly in the eye with a piece of brick.

"That will cost the old man an extra five hundred dollars," says Bill, climbing over the wheel.

That boy put up a fight like a welter-weight cinnamon bear; but, at last, we got him down in the bottom of the buggy and drove away. We took him up to the cave, and I hitched the horse in the cedar brake. After dark I drove the buggy to the little village, three miles away, where we had hired it, and walked back to the mountain.

Bill was pasting court-plaster over the scratches and bruises on his features. There was a fire burning behind the big rock at the entrance of the cave, and the boy was watching a pot of boiling coffee, with two buzzard tail-feathers stuck in his red hair. He points a stick at me when I come up, and says:

"Ha! cursed paleface, do you dare to enter the camp of Red Chief, the terror of the plains?"

"He's all right now," says Bill, rolling up his trousers and examining some bruises on his shins. "We're playing Indian. We're making Buffalo Bill's show look like magic lantern views of Palestine in the town hall. I'm Old Hank, the Trapper, Red Chief's captive, and I'm to be scalped at daybreak. By Geronimo! that kid can kick hard."

Yes, sir, that boy seemed to be having the time of his life. The fun of camping out in a cave had made him forget that he was a captive himself. He immediately christened me Snake-eye, the Spy, and announced that, when his braves returned from the warpath, I was to be broiled at the stake at the rising of the sun.

Then we had supper; and he filled his mouth full of bacon and bread and gravy, and began to talk. He made a during-dinner speech something like this:

"I like this fine. I never camped out before; but I had a pet 'possum once, and I was nine last birthday. I hate to go to school. Rats ate up sixteen of Jimmy Talbot's aunt's speckled hen's eggs. Are there any real Indians in these woods? I want some more gravy. Does the trees moving make the wind blow? We had five puppies. What makes your nose so red, Hank? My father has lots of money. Are the stars hot? I whipped Ed Walker twice, Saturday. I don't like girls. You dassent catch toads unless with a string. Do oxen make any noise? Why are oranges round? Have you got beds to sleep on in this cave? Amos Murray has got six toes. A parrot can talk, but a monkey or a fish can't. How many does it take to make twelve?"

Every few minutes he would remember that he was a pesky redskin, and pick up his stick rifle and tiptoe to the mouth of the cave to rubber for the scouts of the hated paleface. Now and then he would let out a war-whoop that made Old Hank the Trapper shiver. That boy had Bill terrorized from the start.

"Red Chief," says I to the kid, "would you like to go home?"

"Aw, what for?" says he. "I don't have any fun at home. I hate to go to school. I like to camp out. You won't take me back home again, Snake-eye, will you?"

"Not right away," says I. "We'll stay here in the cave awhile."

"All right!" says he. "That'll be fine. I never had such fun in all my life."

We went to bed about eleven o'clock. We spread down some wide blankets and quilts and put Red Chief between us. We weren't afraid he'd run away. He kept us awake for three hours, jumping up and reaching for his rifle and screeching: "Hist!

85

pard," in mine and Bill's ears, as the fancied crackle of a twig or the rustle of a leaf revealed to his young imagination the stealthy approach of the outlaw band. At last, I fell into a troubled sleep, and dreamed that I had been kidnapped and chained to a tree by a ferocious pirate with red hair.

Just at daybreak, I was awakened by a series of awful screams from Bill. They weren't yells, or howls, or shouts, or whoops, or yawps, such as you'd expect from a manly set of vocal organs—they were simply indecent, terrifying, humilating screams, such as women emit when they see ghosts or caterpillars. It's an awful thing to hear a strong, desperate, fat man scream incontinently in a cave at daybreak.

I jumped up to see what the matter was. Red Chief was sitting on Bill's chest, with one hand twined his Bill's hair. In the other he had the sharp caseknife we used for slicing bacon; and he was industriously and realistically trying to take Bill's scalp, according to the sentence that had been pronounced upon him the evening before.

I got the knife away from the kid and made him lie down again. But, from that moment, Bill's spirit was broken. He laid down on his side of the bed, but he never closed an eye again in sleep as long as that boy was with us. I dozed off for a while, but along toward sun-up I remembered that Red Chief had said I was to be burned at the stake at the rising of the sun. I wasn't nervous or afraid; but I sat up and lit my pipe and leaned against a rock.

"What you getting up so soon for, Sam?" asked Bill.

"Me?" says I. "Oh, I got a kind of pain in my shoulder. I thought sitting up would rest it."

"You're a liar!" says Bill. "You're afraid. You was to be burned at sunrise, and you was afraid he'd do it. And he would, too, if he could find a match. Ain't it awful, Sam? Do you think anybody will pay out money to get a little imp like that back home?"

"Sure," said I. "A rowdy kid like that is just the kind that parents dote on. Now, you and the Chief get up and cook breakfast, while I go up on the top of this mountain and reconnoitre."

I went up on the peak of the little mountain and ran my eye over the contiguous vicinity. Over towards Summit I expected to see the sturdy yeomanry of the village armed with scythes and pitchforks beating the countryside for the dastardly kidnappers. But what I saw was a peaceful landscape dotted with one man ploughing with a dun mule.

Nobody was dragging the creek; no couriers dashed hither and yon, bringing tidings of no news to the distracted parents. There was a sylvan attitude of somnolent sleepiness pervading that section of the external outward surface of Alabama that lay exposed to my view. "Perhaps," says I to myself, "it has not yet been discovered that the wolves have borne away the tender lambkin from the fold. Heaven help the wolves!" says I, and I went down the mountain to breakfast.

When I got to the cave I found Bill backed up against the side of it, breathing hard, and the boy threatening to smash him with a rock half as big as a cocoanut.

"He put a red-hot boiled potato down my back," explained Bill, "and then mashed it with his foot; and I boxed his ears. Have you got a gun about you, Sam?"

I took the rock away from the boy and kind of patched up the argument. "I'll fix you," says the kid to Bill. "No man ever yet struck the Red Chief but he got paid for it. You better beware!"

After breakfast the kid takes a piece of leather with strings wrapped around it out of his pocket and goes outside the cave unwinding it.

"What's he up to now?" says Bill, anxiously. "You don't think he'll run away, do you, Sam?"

"No fear of it," says I. "He don't seem to be much of a home body. But we've got to fix up some plan about the ransom. There don't seem to be much excitement around Summit on account of his disappearance; but maybe they haven't realized yet that he's gone. His folks may think he's spending the night with Aunt Jane or one of the neighbors. Anyhow, he'll be missed to-day. To-night we must get a message to his father demanding the two thousand dollars for his return."

Just then we heard a kind of war-whoop, such as David might have emitted when he knocked out the champion Goliath. It was a sling that Red Chief had pulled out of his pocket, and he was whirling it around his head.

I dodged, and heard a heavy thud and a kind of a sigh from Bill, like a horse gives out when you take his saddle off. A niggerhead rock the size of an egg had caught Bill just behind his left ear. He loosened himself all over and fell in the fire across the frying pan of hot water for washing the dishes. I dragged him out and poured cold water on his head for half an hour.

By and by, Bill sits up and feels behind his ear

and says: "Sam, do you know who my favorite Biblical character is?"

"Take it easy," says I. "You'll come to your senses presently."

"King Herod," says he. "You won't go away and leave me here alone, will you, Sam?"

I went out and caught that boy and shook him until his freckles rattled.

"If you don't behave," says I, "I'll take you straight home. Now, are you going to be good or not?"

"I was only funning," says he, sullenly. "I didn't mean to hurt Old Hank. But what did he hit me for? I'll behave, Snake eye, if you won't send me home, and if you'll let me play the Black Scout to-day."

"I don't know the game," says I. "That's for you and Mr. Bill to decide. He's your playmate for the day. I'm going away for a while, on business. Now, you come in and make friends with him and say you are sorry for hurting him, or home you go, at once."

I made him and Bill shake hands, and then I took Bill aside and told him I was going to Poplar Cove, a little village three miles from the cave, and find out what I could about how the kidnapping had been regarded in Summit. Also, I thought it best to send a peremptory letter to old man Dorset that day, demanding the ransom and dictating how it should be paid.

"You know, Sam," says Bill, "I've stood by you without batting an eye in earthquakes, fire and flood—in poker games, dynamite outrages, police raids, train robberies, and cyclones. I never lost my nerve yet till we kidnapped that two-legged sky-rocket of a kid. He's got me going. You won't leave me long with him, will you, Sam?"

"I'll be back some time this afternoon," says I. "You must keep the boy amused and quiet till I return. And now we'll write the letter to old Dorset."

Bill and I got paper and pencil and worked on the letter while Red Chief, with a blanket wrapped around him, strutted up and down, guarding the mouth of the cave. Bill begged me tearfully to make the ransom fifteen hundred dollars instead of two thousand. "I ain't attempting," says he, "to decry the celebrated moral aspect of parental affection, but we're dealing with humans, and it ain't human for anybody to give up two thousand dollars for that forty-pound chunk of freckled wildcat. I'm willing to take a chance at fifteen hundred dollars. You can charge the difference up to me."

91

So, to relieve Bill, I acceded, and we collaborated a letter that ran this way:

EBENEZER DORSET, ESQ.:

We have your boy concealed in a place far from Summit. It is useless for you or the most skilful detectives to attempt to find him. Absolutely, the only terms on which you can have him restored to you are these: We demand fifteen hundred dollars in large bills for his return; the money to be left at midnight to-night at the same spot and in the same box as your reply—as hereinafter described. If you agree to these terms, send your answer in writing by a solitary messenger to-night to half-past eight o'clock. After crossing Owl Creek on the road to Poplar Grove, there are three large trees about a hundred yards apart, close to the fence of the wheat field on the right-hand side. At the bottom of the fence-post, opposite the third tree, will be found a small pasteboard box.

The messenger will place the answer in this box and return immediately to Summit.

If you attempt any treachery or fail to comply with our demand as stated, you will never see your boy again.

If you pay the money as demanded, he will be returned to you safe and well within three hours. These terms are final, and if you do not accede to them no further communication will be attempted.

TWO DESPERATE MEN.

I addressed this letter to Dorset, and put it in my pocket. As I was about to start, the kid comes up to me and says:

"Aw, Snake-eye, you said I could play the Black Scout while you was gone."

"Play it, of course," says I. "Mr. Bill will play with you. What kind of a game is it?"

"I'm the Black Scout," says Red Chief, "and I have to ride to the stockade to warn the settlers that the Indians are coming. I'm tired of playing Indian myself. I want to be the Black Scout."

"All right," says I. "It sounds harmless to me. I guess Mr. Bill will help you foil the pesky savages."

"What am I to do?" asks Bill, looking at the kid suspiciously.

"You are the hoss," says Black Scout. "Get down on your hands and knees. How can I ride to the stockade without a hoss?"

"You'd better keep him interested," said I, "till we get the scheme going. Loosen up."

93

Bill gets down on his all fours, and a look comes in his eye like a rabbit's when you catch it in a trap.

"How far is it to the stockade, kid?" he asks, in a husky manner of voice.

"Ninety miles," says the Black Scout. "And you have to hump yourself to get there on time. Whoa, now!"

The Black Scout jumps on Bill's back and digs his heels in his side.

"For Heaven's sake," says Bill, "hurry back, Sam, as soon as you can. I wish we hadn't made the ransom more than a thousand. Say, you quit kicking me or I'll get up and warm you good."

I walked over to Poplar Cove and sat around the post-office and store, talking with the chaw-bacons that came in to trade. One whiskerando says that he hears Summit is all upset on account of Elder Ebenezer Dorset's boy having been lost or stolen. That was all I wanted to know. I bought some smoking tobacco, referred casually to the price of black-eyed peas, posted my letter surreptitiously, and came away. The postmaster said the mail-carrier would come by in an hour to take the mail on to Summit.

When I got back to the cave Bill and the boy were not to be found. I explored the vicinity of the cave, and risked a yodel or two, but there was no response.

So I lighted my pipe and sat down on a mossy bank to await developments.

In about half an hour I heard the bushes rustle, and Bill wabbled out into the little glade in front of the cave. Behind him was the kid, stepping softly like a scout, with a broad grin on his face. Bill stopped, took off his hat, and wiped his face with a red handkerchief. The kid stopped about eight feet behind him.

"Sam," says Bill, "I suppose you'll think I'm a renegade, but I couldn't help it. I'm a grown person with masculine proclivities and habits of self-defense, but there is a time when all systems of egotism and predominance fail. The boy is gone. I sent him home. All is off. There was martyrs in old times," goes on Bill, "that suffered death rather than give up the particular graft they enjoyed. None of 'em ever was subjugated to such supernatural tortures as I have been. I tried to be faithful to our articles of depredation; but there came a limit."

"What's the trouble, Bill?" I asks him.

"I was rode," says Bill, "the ninety miles to the stockade, not barring an inch. Then, when the settlers was rescued, I was given oats. Sand ain't a palatable substitute. And then, for an hour I had to try to explain to him why there was nothin' in holes, how a road can run both ways, and what makes the grass green. I tell you, Sam, a human can only stand so much. I takes him by the neck of his clothes and drags him down the mountain. On the way he kicks my legs black and blue from the knees down; and I've got to have two or three bites on my thumb and hand cauterized.

"But he's gone"—continues Bill—"gone home. I showed him the road to Summit and kicked him about eight feet nearer there at one kick. I'm sorry we lose the ransom; but it was either that or Bill Driscoll to the madhouse."

Bill is puffing and blowing, but there is a look of ineffable peace and growing content on his rose-pink features.

"Bill," says I, "there isn't any heart disease in your family, is there?"

"No," says Bill, "nothing chronic except malaria and accidents. Why?"

"Then you might turn around," says I, "and have a look behind you.

Bill turns and sees the boy, and loses his complexion and sits down plump on the ground and begins to pluck aimlessly at grass and little sticks. For an hour I was afraid of his mind. And then I told him that my scheme was to put the whole job through immediately and that we would get the ransom and be off with it by midnight if old Dorset fell in which our proposition. So Bill braced up enough to give the kid a weak sort of a smile and a promise to play the Russian in a Japanese war with him as soon as he felt a little better.

I had a scheme for collecting that ransom without danger of being caught by counterplots that ought to commend itself to professional kidnappers. The tree under which the answer was to be left— and the money later on—was close to the road fence with big, bare fields on all sides. If a gang of constables should be watching for any one to come for the note they could see him a long way off crossing the fields or in the road. But no, sirrée! At half-past eight I was up in that tree as well hidden as a tree toad, waiting for the messenger to arrive.

Exactly on time, a half-grown boy rides up the road on a bicycle, locates the pasteboard box at the foot of the fence-post, slips a folded piece of paper into it, and pedals away again back toward Summit.

I waited an hour and then concluded the thing was square. I slid down the tree, got the note, slipped along the fence till I struck the woods, and was back at the cave in another half an hour. I opened the note, got near the lantern, and read it to Bill. It was writen with a pen in a crabbed hand, and the sum and substance of it was this:

TWO DESPERATE MEN.

Gentlemen: I received your letter to-day by post, in regard to the ransom you ask for the return of my son. I think you are a little high in your demands, and I hereby make you a counter-proposition, which I am inclined to believe you will accept. You bring Johnny home and pay me two hundred and fifty dollars in cash, and I agree to take him off your hands. You had better come at night, for the neighbors believe he is lost, and I couldn't be responsible for what they would do to anybody they saw bringing him back.

Very respectfully,
EBENEZER DORSET.

"Great pirates of Penzance," says I; "of all the impudent——"

But I glanced at Bill, and hesitated. He had the most appealing look in his eyes I ever saw on the face of a dumb or a talking brute.

"Sam," says he, "what's two hundred and fifty dollars, after all? We've got the money. One more night of this kid will send me to a bed in Bedlam. Besides being a thorough gentleman, I think Mr. Dorset is a spendthrift for making us such a liberal offer. You ain't going to let the chance go, are you?"

"Tell you the truth, Bill," says I, "this little he ewe lamb has somewhat got on my nerves too. We'll take him home, pay the ransom, and make our getaway."

We took him home that night. We got him to go by telling him that his father had bought a silver-mounted rifle and a pair of moccasins for him, and we were to hunt bears the next day.

It was just twelve o'clock when we knocked at Ebenezer's front door. Just at the moment when I should have been abstracting the fifteen hundred dollars from the box under the tree, according to the original proposition, Bill was counting out two hundred and fifty dollars into Dorset's hand.

When the kid found out we were going to leave him at home he started up a howl like a calliope and fastened himself as tight as a leech to Bill's leg. His father peeled him away gradually, like a porous plaster.

"How long can you hold him?" asks Bill.

"I'm not as strong as I used to be," says old Dorset, "but I think I can promise you ten minutes."

"Enough," says Bill. "In ten minutes I shall cross the Central, Southern, and Middle Western States, and be legging it trippingly for the Canadian border."

And, as dark as it was, and as fat as Bill was, and as good a runner as I am, he was a good mile and a half out of Summit before I could catch up with him.

SOUND AND FURY

PERSONS OF THE DRAMA

MR. PENNE   *An Author*
MISS LORE   *An Amanuensis*

SCENE—*Workroom of* Mr. Penne's *popular novel factory.*

MR. PENNE—Good morning, Miss Lore. Glad to see you so prompt. We should finish that June installment for the *Epoch* to-day. Leverett is crowding me for it. Are you quite ready? We will resume where we left off yesterday. (*Dictates.*) "Kate, with a sigh, rose from his knees, and——"

MISS LORE—Excuse me; you mean "rose from *her* knees," instead of "his," don't you?

MR. PENNE—Er—no—"his," if you please. It is

the love scene in the garden. (*Dictates.*) "Rose from his knees where, blushing with youth's bewitching coyness, she had rested for a moment after Cortland had declared his love. The hour was one of supreme and tender joy. When Kate—scene that Cortland never——"

MISS LORE—Excuse me; but wouldn't it be more grammatical to say "when Kate *saw*," instead of "seen"?

MR. PENNE—The context will explain. (*Dictates.*) "When Kate—scene that Cortland never forgot—came tripping across the lawn it seemed to him the fairest sight that earth had ever offered to his gaze."

MISS LORE—Oh!

MR. PENNE (*dictates*)—"Kate had abandoned herself to the joy of her newfound love so completely that no shadow of her former grief was cast upon it. Cortland, with his arm firmly entwined about her waist, knew nothing of her sighs——"

MISS LORE—Goodness! If he couldn't tell her size with his arm around——

MR. PENNE (*frowning*)—"Of her sighs and tears of the previous night."

MISS LORE—Oh!

MR. PENNE (*dictates*)—"To Cortland the chief

102

charm of this girl was her look of innocence and un-worldliness. Never had nun——"

Miss Lore—How about changing that to "never had any"?

Mr. Penne (*emphatically*)—"Never had nun in cloistered cell a face more sweet and pure."

Miss Lore—Oh!

Mr. Penne (*dictates*)—"But now Kate must hasten back to the house lest her absence be discovered. After a fond farewell she turned and sped lightly away. Cortland's gaze followed her. He watched her rise——"

Miss Lore—Excuse me, Mr. Penne; but how could he watch her eyes while her back was turned toward him?

Mr. Penne (*with extreme politeness*)—Possibly you would gather my meaning more intelligently if you would wait for the conclusion of the sentence. (*Dictates.*) "Watched her rise as gracefully as a fawn as she mounted the eastern terrace."

Miss Lore—Oh!

Mr. Penne (*dictates*)—"And yet Cortland's position was so far above that of this rustic maiden that he dreaded to consider the social upheaval that would ensue should he marry her. In no uncertain tones the traditional voices of his caste and world cried out loudly to him to let her go. What should follow——"

MISS LORE (*looking up with a start*)—I'm sure I can't say, Mr. Penne. Unless (*with a giggle*) you would want to add "Gallegher."

MR. PENNE (*coldly*)—Pardon me. I was not seeking to impose upon you the task of a collaborator. Kindly consider the question of a part of the text.

MISS LORE—Oh!

MR. PENNE (*dictates*)—"On one side was love and Kate; on the other side his heritage of social position and family pride. Would love win? Love, that the poets tell us will last forever!" (*Perceives that* Miss Lore *look fatigued, and looks at his watch.*) That's a good long stretch. Perhaps we'd better knock off a bit.

(Miss Lore *does not reply.*)

MR. PENNE—I said, Miss Lore, we've been at it quite a long time—wouldn't you like to knock off for a while?

MISS LORE—Oh! Were you addressing me before? I put what you said down. I thought it belonged in the story. It seemed to fit in all right. Oh, no; I'm not tired.

MR. PENNE—Very well, then, we will continue. (*Dictates.*) "In spite of these qualms and doubts,

Cortland was a happy man. That night at the club he silently toasted Kate's bright eyes in a bumper of the rarest vintage. Afterward he set out for a stroll with, as Kate on——"

MISS LORE—Excuse me, Mr. Penne, for venturing a suggestion; but don't you think you might state that in a less coarse manner?

MR. PENNE (*astounded*)—Wh-wh—I'm afraid I fail to understand you.

MISS LORE—His condition. Why not say he was "full" or "intoxicated"? It would sound much more elegant than the way you express it.

MR. PENNE (*still darkly wandering*)—Will you kindly point out, Miss Lore, where I have intimated that Cortland was "full," if you prefer that word?

MISS LORE (*calmly consulting her stenographic notes*)—It is right here, word for word. (*Reads.*) "Afterward he set out for a stroll with a skate on."

MR. PENNE (*with peculiar emphasis*)—Ah! And now will you kindly take down the expurgated phrase? (*Dictates.*) "Afterward he set out for a stroll with, as Kate on one occasion had fancifully told him, her spirit leaning upon his arm."

MISS LORE—Oh!

MR. PENNE (*dictates*)—Chapter thirty-four. Heading—"What Kate Found in the Garden." "That fragrant summer morning brought gracious tasks to all. The bees were at the honeysuckle blossoms on the porch. Kate, singing a little song, was training the riotous branches of her favorite woodbine. The sun, himself, had rows——'

MISS LORE—Shall I say "had risen"?

MR. PENNE (*very slowly and with desperate deliberation*)—"The — sun — himself — had — rows — of — blushing — pinks — and — hollyhocks — and — hyacinths — waiting — that — he — might — dry — their — dew-drenched — cups."

MISS LORE—Oh!

MR. PENNE (*dictates*)—"The earliest trolley, scattering the birds from its pathway like some marauding cat, brought Cortland over from Oldport. He had forgoten his fair——"

MISS LORE—Hm! Wonder how he got the conductor to——

MR. PENNE (*very loudly*)—"Forgotten his fair and roseate visions of the night in the practical light of the sober morn."

MISS LORE—Oh!

MR. PENNE (*dictates*)—"He greeted her with his usual smile and manner. 'See the waves,' he cried, pointing to the heaving waters of the sea, 'ever wooing and returning to the rock-bound shore. "'Ready to break,' Kate said, with——"

MISS LORE—My! One evening he has his arm

around her, and the next morning he's ready to break her head! Just like a man!

MR. PENNE (*with suspicious calmness*)—There are times, Miss Lore, when a man becomes so far exasperated that even a woman—— But suppose we finish the sentence. (*Dictates.*) " 'Ready to break,' Kate said, with the thrilling look of a soul-awakened woman, 'into foam and spray, destroying themselves upon the shore they love so well.' "

MISS LORE—Oh!

MR. PENNE (*dictates*)—"Cortland, in Kate's presence heard faintly the voice of caution. Thirty years had not cooled his ardor. It was in his power to bestow great gifts upon this girl. He still retained the beliefs that he had at twenty." (*To* Miss Lore, *wearily*) I think that will be enough for the present.

MISS LORE (*wisely*)—Well, if he had the twenty that he believed he had, it might buy her a rather nice one.

MR. PENNE (*faintly*)—The last sentence was my own. We will discontinue for the day, Miss Lore.

MISS LORE—Shall I come again to-morrow?

MR. PENNE (*helpless under the spell*)—If you will be so good.

(*Exit* Miss Lore.)

ASBESTOS CURTAIN

THE HANDBOOK OF HYMEN

'TIS THE OPINION of myself, Sanderson Pratt, who sets this down, that the educational system of the United States should be in the hands of the weather bureau. I can give you good reasons for it; and you can't tell me why our college professors shouldn't be transferred to the meteorological department. They have been learned to read; and they could very easily glance at the morning papers and then wire in to the main office what kind of weather to expect. But there's the other side of the proposition. I am going on to tell you how the weather furnished me and Idaho Green with an elegant education.

We was up in the Bitter Root Mountains over the Montana line prospecting for gold. A chin-whiskered man in Walla-Walla, carrying a line of hope as excess baggage, had grubstaked us; and there we was in the foothills pecking away, with enough grub on hand to last an army through a peace conference.

Along one day comes a mail-rider over the mountains from Carlos, and stops to eat three cans of green-gages, and leave us a newspaper of modern date. This paper prints a system of premonitions of the weather, and the card it dealt Bitter Root Mountains from the bottom of the deck was "warmer and fair, with light westerly breezes."

That evening it began to snow, with the wind strong in the east. Me and Idaho moved camp into an old empty cabin higher up the mountain, thinking it was only a November flurry. But after falling three foot on a level it went to work in earnest; and we knew we was snowed in. We got in plenty of firewood before it got deep, and we had grub enough for two months, so we let the elements rage and cut up all they thought proper.

If you want to instigate the art of manslaughter just shut two men up in a eighteen by twenty-foot cabin for a month. Human nature won't stand it.

When the first snowflakes fell me and Idaho Green laughed at each other's jokes and praised the stuff we turned out of a skillet and called bread. At the end of three weeks Idaho makes this kind of a edict to me. Says he:

"I never exactly heard sour milk dropping out of a balloon on the bottom of a tin pan, but I have an idea it would be music of the spears compared to this attenuated stream of asphyxiated thought that emanates out of your organs of conversation. The kind of half-masticated noise that you emit every day puts me in mind of a cow's cud, only she's lady enough to keep hers to herself, and you ain't."

"Mr. Green," says I, "you having been a friend of mine once, I have some hesitations in confessing to you that if I had my choice for society between you and a common yellow three-legged cur pup, one of the inmates of this here cabin would be wagging a tail just at present."

This way we goes on for two or three days, and then we quits speaking to one another. We divides up the cooking implements, and Idaho cooks his grub on one side of the fireplace, and me on the other. The snow is up to the windows, and we have to keep a fire all day.

You see me and Idaho never had any education beyond reading and doing "if John had three apples and James five" on a slate. We never felt any special need for a university degree, though we had acquired a species of intrinsic intelligence in knocking around the world that we could use in emergencies. But snowbound in that cabin in the Bitter Roots, we felt for the first time that if we had studied Homer or Greek and fractions and the higher branches of information, we'd have had some resources in the line of meditation and private thought. I've seen them Eastern college fellows working in camps all through the West, and I never noticed but what education was less of a drawback to 'em than you would think. Why, once over on Snake River, when Andrew McWilliams' saddle horse got the botts, he sent a buckboard ten miles for one of these strangers that claimed to be a botanist. But that horse died.

One morning Idaho was poking around with a stick on top of a little shelf that was too high to reach. Two books fell down to the floor. I started toward 'em but caught Idaho's eye. He speaks for the first time in a week.

"Don't burn your fingers," says he. "In spite of the fact that you're only fit to be the companion of a sleeping mud-turtle, I'll give you a square deal. And that's more than your parents did when they turned you loose in the world with the sociability of a rattlesnake and the bedside manner of a frozen turnip. I'll play you a game of seven-up, the winner to pick up his choice of the book, the loser to take the other."

111

We played; and Idaho won. He picked up his book; and I took mine. Then each of us got on his side of the house and went to reading.

I never was as glad to see a ten-ounce nugget as I was that book. And Idaho looked at his like a kid looks at a stick of candy.

Mine was a little book about five by six inches called "Herkimer's Handbook of Indispensable Information." I may be wrong, but I think that was the greatest book that ever was written. I've got it to-day; and I can stump you or any man fifty times in five minutes with the information in it. Talk about Solomon or the New York *Tribune!* Herkimer had cases on both of 'em. That man must have put in fifty years and travelled a million miles to find out all that stuff. There was the population of all cities in it, and the way to tell a girl's age, and the number of teeth a camel has. It told you the longest tunnel in the world, the number of the stars, how long it takes for chicken pox to break out, what a lady's neck ought to measure, the veto powers of Governors, the dates of the Roman aqueducts, how many pounds of rice going without three beers a day would buy, the average annual temperature of Augusta, Maine, the quantity of seed required to plant an acre of carrots in drills, antidotes for poisons, the number of hairs on a blond lady's head, how to preserve eggs, the height of all the mountains in the world, and the dates of all wars and battles, and how to restore drowned persons, and sunstrokes, and the number of tacks in a pound, and how to make dynamite and flowers and beds, and what to do before the doctor comes —and a hundred times as many things besides. If there was anything Herkimer didn't know I didn't miss it out of the book.

I sat and read that book for four hours. All the wonders of education was compressed in it. I forgot the snow, and I forgot that me and old Idaho was on the outs. He was sitting on a stool reading away with a kind of partly soft and partly mysterious look shining through his tan-bark whiskers.

"Idaho," says I, "what kind of a book is yours?"

Idaho must have forgot, too, for he answered moderate, without any slander or malignity.

"Why," says he, "this here seems to be a volume by Homer K. M."

"Homer K. M. what?" I asked.

"Why, just Homer K. M.," says he.

"You're a liar," says I, a little riled that Idaho should try to put me up a tree. "No man is going 'round signing books with his initials. If it's Homer K. M. Spoopendyke, or Homer K. M. McSweeney, or Homer K. M. Jones, why don't you say so like a man instead of biting off the end of it like a calf chewing off the tail of a shirt on a clothes-line?"

"I put it to you straight, Sandy," says Idaho, quiet. "It's a poem book," says he, "by Homer K. M. I couldn't get color out of it at first, but there's a vein if you follow it up. I wouldn't have missed this book for a pair of red blankets."

"You're welcome to it," says I. "What I want is a disinterested statement of facts for the mind to work on, and that's what I seem to find in the book I've drawn."

"What you've got," says Idaho, "is statistics, the lowest grade of information that exists. They'll poison your mind. Give me old K. M.'s system of surmises. He seems to be a kind of a wine agent. His regular toast is 'nothing doing,' and he seems to have a grouch, but he keeps it so well lubricated with booze that his worst kicks sound like an invitation to split a quart. But it's poetry," says Idaho, "and I have sensations of scorn for that truck of yours that tries to convey sense in feet and inches. When it comes to explaining the instinct of philosophy through the art of nature, old K. M. has got your man beat by drills, rows, paragraphs, chest measurement, and average annual rainfall."

So that's the way me and Idaho had it. Day and

night all the excitement we got was studying our books. That snowstorm sure fixed us with a fine lot of attainments apiece. By the time the snow melted, if you had stepped up to me suddenly and said: "Sanderson Pratt, what would it cost per square foot to lay a roof with twenty by twenty-eight tin at nine dollars and fifty cents per box?" I'd have told you as quick as light could travel the length of a spade handle at the rate of one hundred and ninety-two thousand miles per second. How many can do it? You wake up 'most any man you know in the middle of the night, and ask him quick to tell you the number of bones in the human skeleton exclusive of the teeth, or what percentage of the vote of the Nebraska Legislature overrules a veto. Will he tell you? Try him and see.

About what benefit Idaho got out of his poetry book I didn't exactly know. Idaho boosted the wine-agent every time he opened his mouth; but I wasn't so sure.

This Homer K. M., from what leaked out of his libretto through Idaho, seemed to me to be a kind of a dog who looked at life like it was a tin can tied to his tail. After running himself half to death, he sits down, hangs his tongue out, and looks at the can and says:

115

"Oh, well, since we can't shake the growler, let's get it filled at the corner, and all have a drink on me."

Besides that, it seems he was a Persian; and I never hear of Persia producing anything worth mentioning unless it was Turkish rugs and Maltese cats.

That spring me and Idaho struck pay ore. It was a habit of ours to sell out quick and keep moving. We unloaded on our grubstaker for eight thousand dollars apiece; and then we drifted down to this little town of Rosa, on the Salmon River, to rest up, and get some human grub, and have our whiskers harvested.

Rosa was no mining-camp. It laid in the valley, and was as free of uproar and pestilence as one of them rural towns in the country. There was a three-mile trolley line champing its bit in the environs; and me and Idaho spent a week riding on one of the cars, dropping off of nights at the Sunset View Hotel. Being now well read as well as travelled, we was soon *pro re nata* with the best society in Rosa, and was invited to the most dressed-up and high-toned entertainments. It was at a piano recital and quail-eating contest in the city hall, for the benefit of the fire company, that me and Idaho first met Mrs. D. Ormond Sampson, the queen of Rosa society.

Mrs. Sampson was a widow, and owned the only two-story house in town. It was painted yellow, and whichever way you looked from you could see it as plain as egg on the chin of an O'Grady on a Friday. Twenty-two men in Rosa besides me and Idaho was trying to stake a claim on that yellow house.

There was a dance after the song books and quail bones had been raked out of the Hall. Twenty-three of the bunch galloped over to Mrs. Sampson and asked for a dance. I side-stepped the two-step, and asked permission to escort her home. That's where I made a hit.

On the way home says she:

"Ain't the stars lovely and bright to-night, Mr. Pratt?"

"For the chance they've got," says I, "they're humping themselves in a mighty creditable way. That big one you see is sixty-six billions of miles distant. It took thirty-six years for light to reach us. With an eighteen-foot telescope you can see forty-three millions of 'em, including them of the thirteenth magnitude, which, if one was to go out now, you would keep on seeing it for twenty-seven hundred years."

117

"My!" says Mrs. Sampson. "I never knew that before. How warm it is! I'm as damp as I can be from dancing so much."

"That's easy to account for," says I, "when you happen to know that you've got two million sweat-glands working all at once. If every one of your perspiratory ducts, which are a quarter of an inch long, was placed end to end, they would reach a distance of seven miles."

"Lawsy!" says Mrs. Sampson. "It sounds like an irrigation ditch you was describing, Mr. Pratt. How do you get all this knowledge of information?"

"From observation, Mrs. Sampson," I tells her. "I keep my eyes open when I go about the world."

"Mr. Pratt," says she, "I always did admire a man of education. There are so few scholars among the sap-headed plug-uglies of this town that it is a real pleasure to converse with a gentleman of culture. I'd be gratified to have you call at my house whenever you feel so inclined."

And that was the way I got the goodwill of the lady in the yellow house. Every Tuesday and Friday evenings I used to go there and tell her about the wonders of the universe as discovered, tabulated, and complied from nature by Herkimer. Idaho and the other gay Lutherans of the town got every minute of the rest of the week that they could.

I never imagined that Idaho was trying to work on Mrs. Sampson with old K. M.'s rules of courtship till one afternoon when I was on my way over to take her a basket of wild hog-plums. I met the lady coming down the lane that led to her house. Her eyes was snapping, and her hat made a dangerous dip over one eye.

"Mr. Pratt," she opens up, "this Mr. Green is a friend of yours, I believe."

"For nine years," says I.

"Cut him out,' says she. "He's no gentleman!"

"Why, ma'am," says I, "he's a plain incumbent of the mountain, with asperities and the usual failings of a spendthrift and a liar, but I never on the most momentous occasion had the heart to deny that he was a gentleman. It may be that in haberdashery and the sense of arrogance and display Idaho offends the eye, but inside, ma'am, I've found him impervious to the lower grades of crime and obesity. After nine years of Idaho's society, Mrs. Sampson," I winds up, "I should hate to impute him, and I should hate to see him imputed."

"It's right plausible of you, Mr. Pratt," says Mrs. Sampson, "to take up the curmudgeons in your friend's behalf; but it don't alter the fact that he

119

has made proposals to me sufficiently obnoxious to ruffle the ignominy of any lady."

"Why, now, now, now!" says I. "Old Idaho do that! I could believe it of myself sooner. I never knew but one thing to deride in him; and a blizzard was responsible for that. Once while we was snowbound in the mountains he became a prey to a kind of spurious and uneven poetry, which may have corrupted his demeanor."

"It has," says Mrs. Sampson. "Ever since I knew him he has been reciting to me a lot of irreligious rhymes by some person he calls Ruby Ott, and who is no better than she should be, if you judge by her poetry."

"Then Idaho has struck a new book," says I, "for the one he had was by a man who writes under the *nom de plume* of K. M."

"He'd better have stuck to it," says Mrs. Sampson, "whatever it was. And to-day he caps the vortex. I get a bunch of flowers from him, and on 'em is pinned a note. Now, Mr. Pratt, you know a lady when you see her; and you know how I stand in Rosa society. Do you think for a moment that I'd skip out to the woods with a man along with a jug of wine and a loaf of bread, and go singing and cavorting up and down under the trees with him?

I take a little claret with my meals, but I'm not in the habit of packing a jug of it into the brush and raising Cain in any such style as that. And of course he'd bring his book of verses along, too. He said so. Let him go on his scandalous picnics alone! Or let him take his Ruby Ott with him. I reckon she wouldn't kick unless it was on account of there being too much bread along. And what do you think of your gentleman friend now, Mr. Pratt?"

"Well, 'm," says I, "it may be that Idaho's invitation was a kind of poetry, and meant no harm. Maybe it belonged to the class of rhymes they call figurative. They offend law and order, but they get sent through the mails on the grounds that they mean something that they don't say. I'd be glad on Idaho's account if you'd overlook it," say I, "and let us extricate our minds from the low regions of poetry to the higher planes of fact and fancy. On a beautiful afternoon like this, Mrs. Sampson," I goes on, "we should let our thoughts dwell accordingly. Though it is warm here, we should remember that at the equator the line of perpetual frost is at an altitude of fifteen thousand feet. Between the latitudes of forty degrees and forty-nine degrees it is from four thousand to nine thousand feet."

"Oh, Mr. Pratt," says Mrs. Sampson, "it's such

a comfort to hear you say them beautiful facts after getting such a jar from that minx of a Ruby's poetry!"

"Let us sit on this log at the roadside," says I, "and forget the inhumanity and ribaldry of the poets. It is in the glorious columns of ascertained facts and legalized measures that beauty is to be found. In this very log we sit upon, Mrs. Sampson," says I, "is statistics more wonderful than any poem. The rings show it was sixty years old. At the depth of two thousand feet it yould become coal in three thousand years. The deepest coal mine in the world is at Killingworth, near Newcastle. A box four feet long, three feet wide, and two feet eight inches deep will hold one ton of coal. If an artery is cut, compress it above the wound. A man's leg contains thirty bones. The Tower of London was burned in 1841."

"Go on, Mr. Pratt," says Mrs. Sampson. "Them ideas is so original and soothing. I think statistics are just as lovely as they can be."

But it wasn't till two weeks later that I got all that was coming to me out of Herkimer.

One night I was waked up by folks hollering "Fire!" all around. I jumped up and dressed and went out of the hotel to enjoy the scene. When I seen it was Mrs. Sampson's house, I gave forth a kind of yell, and I was there in two minutes.

The whole lower story of the yellow house was in flames, and every masuline, feminine, and canine in Rosa was there, screeching and barking and getting in the way of the firemen. I saw Idaho trying to get away from six firemen who were holding him. They was telling him the whole place was on fire downstairs, and no man could go in it and come out alive.

"Where's Mrs. Sampson?" I asks.

"She hasn't been seen," says one of the firemen. "She sleeps upstairs. We've tried to get in, but we can't, and our company hasn't got any ladders yet."

I runs around to the light of the big blaze, and pulls the Handbook out of my inside pocket. I kind of laughed when I felt it in my hands—I reckon I was some daffy with the sensation of excitement.

"Herky, old boys," I says to it, as I flipped over the pages, "you ain't ever lied to me yet, and you ain't ever throwed me down at a scratch yet. Tell me what, old boy, tell me what!" says I.

I turned to "What to do in Case of Accidents," on page 117. I run my finger down the page, and struck it. Good old Herkimer, he never overlooked anything! It said:

123

SUFFOCATION FROM INHALING SMOKE OR GAS.—
There is nothing better than flaxseed. Place a few
seed in the outer corner of the eye.

I shoved the Handbook back in my pocket, and
grabbed a boy that was running by.

"Here," says I, giving him some money, "run to
the drug store and bring a dollars' worth of flaxseed. Hurry, and you'll get another one for yourself. Now," I sings out to the crowd, "we'll have
Mrs. Sampson!" And I throws away my coat and
hat.

Four of the firemen and citizens grabs hold of me.
It's sure death, they say, to go in the house, for
the floors was beginning to fall through.

"How in blazes," I sings out, kind of laughing
yet, but not feeling like it, "do you expect me to
put flaxseed in a eye without the eye?"

I jabbed each elbow in a fireman's face, kicked
the bark off of one citizen's shin, and tripped the
other one with a side hold. And then I busted into
the house. If I die first I'll write you a letter and
tell you if it's any worse down there than the inside
of that yellow house was; but don't believe it yet.
I was a heap more cooked than the hurry-up orders
of broiled chicken that you get in restaurants. The
fire and smoke had me down on the floor twice,

and was about to shame Herkimer, but the firemen helped me with their little stream of water, and I got to Mrs. Sampson's room. She'd lost conscientiousness from the smoke, so I wrapped her in the bed clothes and got her on my shoulder. Well, the floors wasn't as bad as they said, or I never could have done it—not by no means.

I carried her out fifty yards from the house and laid her on the grass. Then, of course, every one of them other twenty-two plaintiffs to the lady's hand crowded around with tin dippers of water to save her. And up runs the boy with the flaxseed.

I unwrapped the covers from Mrs. Sampson's head. She opened her eyes and says:

"Is that you, Mr. Pratt?"

"S-s-sh," says I. "Don't talk till you've had the remedy."

I runs my arm around her neck and raises her head, gentle, and breaks the bag of flaxseed with the other hand; and as easy as I could I bends over and slips three or four of the seeds in the outer corner of her eye.

Up gallops the village doc by this time, and snorts around, and grabs at Mrs. Sampson's pulse, and wants to know what I mean by any such sand-blasted nonsense.

125

"Well, old Jalap and Jerusalem oak seed," says I, "I'm no regular practitioner, but I'll show you my authority, anyway."

They fetched my coat, and I gets out the Handbook.

"Look on page 117," says I "at the remedy for suffocation by smoke or gas. Flaxseed in the outer corner of the eye, it says. I don't know whether it works as a smoke consumer or whether it hikes the compound gastro-hippopotamus nerve into action, but Herkimer says it, and he was called to the case first. If you want to make it a consultation, there's no objection."

Old doc takes the book and looks at it by means of his specs and a fireman's lantern.

"Well, Mr. Pratt," says he, "you evidently got on the wrong line in reading your diagnosis. The recipe for suffocation says: "Get the patient into fresh air as quickly as possible, and place in a reclining position.' The flaxseed remedy is for 'Dust and Cinders in the Eye,' on the line above. But, after all——"

"See here," interrupts Mrs. Sampson, "I reckon I've got something to say in this consultation. That flaxseed done me more good than anything I ever tried." And then she raises up her head and lays it back on my arm again, and says: "Put some in the other eye, Sandy dear."

And so if you was to stop off at Rosa to-morrow, or any other day, you'd see a fine new yellow house with Mrs. Pratt, that was Mrs. Sampson, embellishing and adorning it. And if you was to step inside you'd see on the marble-top centre table in the parlor, "Herkimer's Handbook of Indispensable Information," all rebound in red morocco, and ready to be consulted on any subject pertaining to human happiness and wisdom.

THE HALBERDIER OF
THE LITTLE RHEINSCHLOSS

Go SOMETIMES into the *Bierhalle* and restaurant called Old Munich. Not long ago it was a resort of interesting Bohemians, but now only artists and musicians and literary folk frequent it. But the Pilsener is yet good, and I take some diversion from the conversation of Waiter No. 18.

For many years the customers of Old Munich have accepted the place as a faithful copy from the ancient German town. The big hall with its smoky rafters, rows of imported steins, portrait of Goethe, and verses painted on the walls—translated into German from the original of the Cincinnati poets —seems atmospherically correct when viewed through the bottom of a glass.

But not long ago the proprietors added the room above, called it the Little Rheinschloss, and built in a stairway. Up there was an imitation stone parapet, ivy-covered, and the walls were painted to represent depth and distance, with the Rhine winding at the base of the vineyarded slopes, and the castle of Ehrenbreitstein looming directly opposite the entrance. Of course there were tables and chairs; and you could have beer and food brought you, as you naturally would on the top of a castle on the Rhine.

I went into Old Munich one afternoon when there were few customers, and sat at my usual table near the stairway. I was shocked and almost displeased to perceive that the glass cigar-case by the orchestra stand had been smashed to smithereens. I did not like things to happen in Old Munich. Nothing had ever happened there before.

Waiter No. 18 came and breathed on my neck. I was his by right of discovery. Eighteen's brain was built like a corral. It was full of ideas which, when he opened the gate, came huddling out like a flock of sheep that might get together afterward or might not. I did not shine as a shepherd. As a type Eighteen fitted nowhere. I did not find out if he had a nationality, family, creed, grievance, hobby, soul, preference, home, or vote. He only came always to my table and, as long as his leisure would permit, let words flutter from him like swallows leaving a barn at daylight.

"How did the cigar-case come to be broken, Eighteen?" I asked, with a certain feeling of personal grievance.

"I can tell you about that, sir," said he, resting his foot on the chair next to mine. "Did you ever have anybody hand you a double handful of good luck while both your hands was full of bad luck, and stop to notice how your fingers behaved?"

"No riddles, Eighteen," said I. "Leave out palmistry and manicuring."

"You remember," said Eighteen, "the guy in the hammered brass Prince Albert and the oroide gold pants and the amalgamated copper hat, that carried the combination meat-axe, ice-pick, and liberty-pole, and used to stand on the first landing as you go up to the Little Rindslosh?"

"Why, yes," said I. "The halberdier. I never noticed him particularly. I remember I thought he was only a suit of armour. He had a perfect poise."

"He had more than that," said Eighteen. "He was me friend. He was an advertisement. The boss hired him to stand on the stairs for a kind of scenery to show there was something doing in the has-been line upstairs. What did you call him—a what kind of beer?"

"A halberdier," said I. "That was an ancient man-at-arms of many hundred years ago."

"Some mistake," said Eighteen. "This one wasn't that old. He wasn't over twenty-three or four."

"It was the boss's idea, rigging a man up in an ante-bellum suit of tinware and standing him on the landing of the slosh. He bought the goods at a Fourth Avenue antique store, and hung a sign out: 'Able-bodied hal—halberdier wanted. Costume furnished.'

"The same morning a young man with wrecked good clothes and a hungry look comes in, bringing the sign with him. I was filling the mustard-pots at my station.

" 'I'm it,' says he, 'whatever it is. But I never halberdiered in a restaurant. Put me on. Is it a masquerade?'

" 'I hear talk in the kitchen of a fishball,' says I.

" 'Bully for you, Eighteen,' says he. 'You and I'll get on. Show me the boss's desk.'

"Well, the boss tries the Harveyized pajamas on him, and they fitted him like the scales on a baked redsnapper, and he gets the job. You've seen what it is—he stood straight up in the corner of the first landing with his halberd to his shoulder, looking right ahead and guarding the Portugals of the castle. The boss is nutty about having the true Old-World flavor to his joint. 'Halberdiers goes with Rindsloshes,' says he, 'just as rats goes with rathskellers and white cotton stockings with Tyrolean villages.' The boss is a kind of a antiologist, and is all posted upon data and such information.

"From 8 P. M. to two in the morning was the Halberdier's hours. He got two meals with us help and a dollar a night. I eat with him at the table. He liked me. He never told his name. He was traveling impromptu, like kings, I guess. The first time at supper I says to him. 'Have some more of the spuds, Mr. Frelinghuysen.' 'Oh, don't be so formal, and offish, Eighteen,' says he. 'Call me Hal—that's short for halberdier.' 'Oh, don't think I wanted to pry for names,' says I. 'I know all about the dizzy fall from wealth and greatness. We've got a count washing dishes in the kitchen; and the third bartender used to be a Pullman conductor. And they *work*, Sir Percival,' says I, sarcastic.

" 'Eighteen,' says he, 'as a friendly devil in a cabbage-scented hell, would you mind cutting up this piece of steak for me? I don't say that it's got more muscle than I have, but—— And then he shows me the insides of his hands. They were blistered and cut and corned and swelled up till they looked like a couple of flank steaks criss-crossed with a

132

knife—the kind the butchers hide and take home, knowing what is the best.

" 'Shoveling coal,' says he, 'and piling bricks and loading drays. But they gave out, and I had to resign. I was born for a halberdier, and I've been educated for twenty-four years to fill the position. Now, quit knocking my profession, and pass along a lot more of that ham. I'm holding the closing exercises,' says he, 'of a forty-eight-hour fast.'

"The second night he was on the job he walks down from his corner to the cigar-case and calls for cigarettes. The customers at the tables all snicker out loud to show their acquaintance with history. The boss is on.

" 'An'—let's see—oh, yes—'An anarchism,' says the boss. 'Cigarettes was not made at the time when halberdiers was invented.'

" 'The ones you sell was,' says Sir Percival. 'Caporal wins from chronology by the length of a cork tip.' So he gets 'em and lights one, and puts the box in his brass helmet and goes back to patrolling the Rindslosh.

"He made a big hit, 'specially with the ladies. Some of 'em would poke him with their fingers to see if he was real or only a kind of a stuffed figure they burn in elegy. And when he'd move they'd squeak, and make eyes at him as they went up to

133

the slosh. He looked fine in his halberdashery. He slept at $2 a week in a hall-room on Third Avenue. He invited me up there one night. He had a little book on the washstand that he read instead of shopping in the saloons after hours. 'I'm on to that,' says I, 'from reading about it in novels. All the heroes on the bum carry the little book. It's either Tantalus or Liver or Horace, and it's printed in Latin, and you're a college man. And I wouldn't be surprised,' says I, "if you wasn't educated, too.' But it was only the batting averages of the League for the last ten years.

"One night, about half-past eleven, there comes in a party of these high-rollers that are always hunting up new places to eat in and poke fun at. There was a swell girl in a 40 H.-P. auto tan coat and veil, and a fat old man with white side-whiskers, and a young chap that couldn't keep his feet off the tail of the girl's coat, and an oldish lady that looked upon life as immoral and unnecessary. 'How perfectly delightful,' they says, 'to sup in a slosh.' Up the stairs they go; and in half a minute back down comes the girl, her skirts swishing like the waves on the beach. She stops on the landing and looks our halberdier in the eye.

" 'You!' she says, with a smile that reminded me

134

of lemon sherbet. I was waiting upstairs in the slosh, then, and I was right down here by the door, putting some vinegar and cayenne into an empty bottle of tabasco, and I heard all they said.

" 'It,' says Sir Percival, without moving. 'I'm only local color. Are my hauberk, helmet, and halberd on straight?"

" 'Is there any explanation to this?' says she. 'Is it a practical joke such as men play in those Griddle-cake and Lamb Clubs? I'm afraid I don't see the point. I heard, vaguely, that you were away. For three months I—we have not seen you or heard from you.'

" 'I'm halberdiering for my living,' says the statue. 'I'm working,' says he. 'I don't suppose you know what work means.'

" 'Have you—have you lost your money?' she asks.

"Sir Percival studies a minute.

" 'I am poorer,' says he, 'than the poorest sandwich man on the streets—if I don't earn my living.'

" 'You call this work?' says she. 'I thought a man worked with his hands or his head instead of becoming a mountebank.'

" 'The calling of a halberdier,' says he, 'is an ancient and honorable one. Sometimes,' says he, 'the man-at-arms at the door has saved the castle while the plumed knights were cake-walking in the banquet-halls above.'

" 'I see you're not ashamed,' says she, 'of your peculiar tastes. I wonder, though, that the manhood I used to think I saw in you didn't prompt you to draw water or hew wood instead of publicly flaunting your ignominy in this graceful masquerade.'

"Sir Percival kind of rattles his armor and says: 'Helen, will you suspend sentence in this matter for just a little while? You don't understand,' says he. 'I've got to hold this job down a bit longer.'

" 'You like being a harlequin—or halberdier, as you call it?" says she.

" 'I wouldn't get thrown out of the job just now,' says he, with a grin, 'to be appointed Minister to the Court of St. James's.'

"And then the 40 H.-P. girl's eyes sparkled as hard as diamonds.

" 'Very well,' says she. 'You shall have full run of your serving-man's tastes this night.' And she swims over to the boss's desk and gives him a smile that knocks the specks off his nose.

" 'I think your Rindslosh,' says she, "is as beautiful as a dream. It is a little slice of the Old World set down in New York. We shall have a nice supper up there; but if you will grant us one favor the illusion will be perfect—give us your halberdier to wait on our table.'

"That hit the boss's antiology hobby just right. 'Sure,' says he, 'dot vill be fine. Und der orchestra shall blay "Die Wacht am Rhein" all der time.' And he goes over and tells the halberdier to go upstairs and hustle the grub at the swells' table.

" 'I'm on the job,' says Sir Percival, taking off his helmet and hanging it on his halberd and leaning 'em in the corner. The girl goes up and takes her seat and I see her jaw squared tight under her smile. 'We're going to be waited on by a real halberdier,' says she, 'one who is proud of his profession. Isn't it sweet?'

" 'Ripping,' says the swell young man. 'Much prefer a waiter,' says the fat old gent. 'I hope he doesn't come from a cheap museum,' says the old lady; 'he might have microbes in his costume.'

"Before he goes to the table, Sir Percival takes me by the arm. 'Eighteen,' says he, 'I've got to pull off this job without a blunder. You coach me straight or I'll take that halberd and make hash out of you.' And then he goes up to the table with his coat of mail on and a napkin over his arm and waits for the order.

" 'Why, it's Deering!' says the young swell. 'Hello, old man. What the——'

" 'Beg pardon, sir,' interrupts the halberdier, 'I'm waiting on the table.'

"The old man looks at him grim, like a Boston bull. 'So, Deering,' he says, 'you're at work yet.'

" 'Yes, sir,' says Sir Percival, quiet and gentlemanly as I could have been myself, 'for almost three months, now.' 'You haven't been discharged during the time?' asks the old man. 'Not once, sir,' says he, 'though I've had to change my work several times.'

" 'Waiter,' orders the girl, short and sharp, 'another napkin.' He brings her one, respectful.

"I never saw more devil, if I may say it, stirred up in a lady. There was two bright red spots on her cheeks, and her eyes looked exactly like a wildcat's I'd seen in the zoo. Her foot kept slapping the floor all the time.

" 'Waiter,' she orders, 'bring me filtered water without ice. Bring me a footstool. Take away this empty salt-cellar.' She kept him on the jump. She was sure giving the halberdier his.

" 'There wasn't but a few customers up in the slosh at that time, so I hung out near the door so I could help Sir Percival serve.

138

"He got along fine with the olives and celery and the bluepoints. That was easy. And then the con-sommé came up the dumb-waiter all in one big silver tureen. Instead of serving it from the side-table he picks it up between his hands and starts to the dining-table with it. When nearly there he drops the tureen smash on the floor, and the soup soaks all the lower part of that girl's swell silk dress.

" 'Stupid—incompetent,' says she, giving him a look. 'Standing in a corner with a halberd seems to be your mission in life.'

" 'Pardon me, lady,' says he. 'It was just a little bit hotter than blazes. I couldn't help it.'

"The old man pulls out a memorandum book and hunts in it. 'The 25th of April, Deering,' says he. 'I know it,' says Sir Percival. 'And ten minutes to twelve o'clock,' says the old man. 'By Jupiter! you haven't won yet.' And he pounds the table with his fist and yells to me: 'Waiter, call the manager at once—tell him to hurry here as fast as he can.' I go after the boss and old Brockman hikes up to the slosh on the jump.

" 'I want this man discharged at once,' roars the old guy. 'Look what he's done. Ruined my daugh-ter's dress. It cost at least $600. Discharge this awkward lout at once or I'll sue you for the price of it.'

" 'Dis is bad pizness,' says the boss. 'Six hundred dollars is much. I reckon I vill haf to——'

" 'Wait a minute, Herr Brockmann,' says Sir Percival, easy and smiling. But he was worked up under his tin suitings; I could see that. And then he made the finest, neatest little speech I ever listened to. I can't give you the words, of course. He gives the millionaires a lovely roast in a sarcastic way, describing their automobiles and opera-boxes and diamonds; and then he got around to the working-classes and the kind of grub they eat and the long hours they work—and all that sort of stuff—bunkum, of course. "The restless rich," says he, 'never content with their luxuries, always prowling among the haunts of the poor and humble, amusing themselves with the imperfections and misfortunes of their fellow men and women. And even here, Herr Brockmann,' he says, 'in this beautiful Rindslosh, a grand and enlightening reproduction of Old-World history and architecture, they come to disturb its symmetry and picturesqueness by demanding in their arrogance that the halberdier of the castle wait upon their table! I have faithfully and conscientiously,' says he, 'performed my duties as a halberdier. I know nothing of a waiter's duties. It was the insolent whim of these transient, pampered aristocrats that I should be detailed to serve them food. Must I be blamed—must I be deprived of the means of a livelihood,' he goes on, 'on account of an accident that was the result of their own presumption and haughtiness? But what hurts me more than all,' says Sir Percival, 'is the desecration that has been done to this splendid Rindslosh—the confiscation of its halberdier to serve menially at the banquet board.'

"Even I could see that this stuff was piffle; but it caught the boss.

"'Mein Gott,' says he 'you vas right. Ein halberdier have not got der right to dish up soup. Him I vill not discharge. Have anoder waiter if you like, and let mein halberdier go back and stand mit his halberd. But, gentlemen,' he says, pointing to the old man, 'you go ahead and sue mit der dress. Sue me for $600 or $6,000. I stand der suit.' And the boss puffs off downstairs. Old Brockman was an all-right Dutchman.

"Just then the clock strikes twelve, and the old guy laughs loud. 'You win, Deering,' says he. 'Let me explain to all,' he goes on. 'Some time ago Mr. Deering asked me for something that I did not want to give him.' (I looks at the girl, and she turns as red as a pickled beet.) 'I told him,' says the old guy, 'if he would earn his own living for three months without once being discharged for incompetence, I would give him what he wanted. It seems that the time was up at twelve o'clock tonight. I came near fetching you, though, Deering, on that soup question," says the old boy, standing up and grabbing Sir Percival's hand.

"The halberdier lets out a yell and jumps three feet high.

" 'Look out for those hands,' say he, and he holds 'em up. You never saw such hands except on a laborer in a limestone quarry.

" 'Heavens, boy!' says old side-whiskers, 'what have you been doing to 'em?'

" 'Oh,' says Sir Percival, 'little chores like hauling coal and excavating rock till they went back on me. And when I couldn't hold a pick or a whip I took up halberdiering to give 'em a rest. Tureens full of hot soup don't seem to be a particularly soothing treatment.'

"I would have bet on that girl. That high-tempered kind always go as far the other way, according to my experience. She whizzes round the table like a cyclone and catches both his hands in hers. 'Poor hands—dear hands,' she sings out, and sheds tears on 'em and holds 'em close to her bosom. Well, sir, with all that Rindslosh scenery it was just like a play. And the halberdier sits down at the table at the girl's side, and I served the rest of the super. And that was about, all, except that when they left he shed his hardware store and went with 'em."

I dislike to be side-tracked from an original prop-osition.

"But you haven't told me, Eighteen," said I, "how the cigar-case came to be broken."

"Oh, that was last night," said Eighteen. "Sir Percival and the girl drove up in a cream-colored motor-car, and had dinner in the Rindslosh. "The same table, Billy,' I heard her say as they went up. I waited on 'em. We've got a new halberdier now, a bow-legged guy with a face like a sheep. As they came downstairs Sir Percival passes him a ten-case note. The new halberdier drops his halberd, and it falls on the cigar-case. That's how that happened."

THE DEFEAT OF THE CITY

ROBERT WALMSLEY'S descent upon the city resulted in a Kilkenny struggle. He came out of the fight victor by a fortune and a reputation. On the other hand, he was swallowed up by the city. The city gave him what he demanded and then branded him with its brand. It remodelled, cut, trimmed, and stamped him to the pattern it approves. It opened its social gates to him and shut him in on a close-cropped, formal lawn with the select herd of ruminants. In dress, habits, manners, provincialism, routine, and narrowness he acquired that charming insolence, that irritating completeness, that sophisticated crassness, that over-balanced poise that makes the Manhattan gentleman so delightfully small in his greatness.

One of the up-state rural counties pointed with

pride to the successful young metropolitan lawyer as a product of its soil. Six years earlier this country had removed the wheat straw from between its huckleberry-stained teeth and emitted a derisive and bucolic laugh as old man Walmsley's freckle-faced "Bob" abandoned the certain three-per-diem meals of the one-horse farm for the discontinuous quick lunch counters of the three-ringed metropolis. At the end of the six years no murder trial, coaching party, automobile accident or cotillion was complete in which the name Robert Walmsley did not figure. Tailors waylaid him in the street to get a new wrinkle from the cut of his unwrinkled trousers. Hyphenated fellows in the clubs and members of the oldest subpœnaed families were glad to clap him on the back and allow him three letters of his name.

But the Matterhorn of Robert Walmsley's success was not scaled until he married Alicia Van Der Pool. I cite the Matterhorn, for just so high and cool and white and inaccessible was this daughter of the old burghers. The social Alps that ranged about her—over whose bleak passes a thousand climbers struggled—reached only to her knees. She towered in her own atmosphere, serene, chaste, prideful, wading in no fountains, dining no monk-

145

eys, breeding no dogs for bench shows. She was a Van Der Pool. Fountains were made to play for her; monkeys were made for other people's ancestors; dogs, she understood, were created to be companions of blind persons and objectionable characters who smoked pipes.

This was the Mattterhorn that Robert Walmsley accomplished. If he found, with the good poet with the game foot and artificially curled hair, that he who ascends to mountain tops will find the loftiest peaks most wrapped in clouds and snow, he concealed his chilblains beneath a brave and smiling exterior. He was a lucky man and knew it, even though he were imitating the Spartan boy with an ice-cream freezer beneath his doublet frappéeing the region of his heart.

After a brief wedding tour abroad, the couple returned to create a decided ripple in the calm cistern (so placid and cool and sunless it is) of the best society. They entertained at their red brick mausoleum of ancient greatness in an old square that is a cemetery of crumbled glory. And Robert Walmsley was proud of his wife; although while one of his hands shook his guests' the other held tightly to his alpenstock and thermometer.

One day Alicia found a letter written to Robert

146

by his mother. It was an unerudite letter, full of crops and motherly love and farm notes. It chronicled the health of the pig and the recent red calf, and asked concerning Robert's in return. It was a letter direct from the soil, straight from home, full of biographies of bees, tales of turnips, pæans of new-laid eggs, neglected parents and the slump in dried apples.

"Why have I not been shown your mother's letters?" asked Alicia. There was always something in her voice that made you think of lorgnettes, of accounts at Tiffany's, of sledges smoothly gliding on the trail from Dawson to Forty Mile, of the tinkling of pendent prisms on your grandmothers' chandeliers, of snow lying on a convent roof; of a police sergeant refusing bail. "Your mother," continued Alicia, "invites us to make a visit to the farm. I have never seen a farm. We will go there for a week or two, Robert."

"We will," said Robert, with the grand air of an associate Supreme Justice concurring in an opinion. "I did not lay the invitation before you because I thought you would not care to go. I am much pleased at your decision."

"I will write to her myself," answered Alicia, with a faint foreshadowing of enthusiasm. "Félice shall pack my trunks at once. Seven, I think, will be enough. I do not suppose that your mother entertains a great deal. Does she give many house parties?"

Robert arose, and as attorney for rural places filed a demurrer against six of the seven trunks. He endeavored to define, picture, elucidate, set forth and describe a farm. His own words sounded strange in his ears. He had not realized how thoroughly urbsidized he had become.

A week passed and found them landed at the little country station five hours out from the city. A grinning, stentorian, sarcastic youth driving a mule to a spring wagon hailed Robert savagely.

"Hallo, Mr. Walmsley. Found your way back at last, have you? Sorry I couldn't bring in the automobile for you, but dat's bull-tonguing the ten-acre clover patch with it to-day. Guess you'll excuse my not wearing a dress suit over to meet you—it ain't six o'clock yet, you know."

"I'm glad to see you, Tom," said Robert, grasping his brother's hand. "Yes, I've found my way at last. You've a right to say 'at last.' It's been over two years since the last time. But it will be oftener after this, my boy."

Alicia, cool in the summer heat as an Arctic

wraith, white as a Norse snow maiden in her flimsy muslin and fluttering lace parasol, came round the corner of the station; and Tom was stripped of his assurance. He became chiefly eyesight clothed in blue jeans, and on the homeward drive to the mule alone did he confide in language the inwardness of his thoughts.

They drove homeward. The low sun dropped a spendthrift flood of gold upon the fortunate fields of wheat. The cities were far away. The road lay curling around wood and dale and hill like a ribbon lost from the robe of careless summer. The wind followed like a whinnying colt in the track of Phœbus's steeds.

By and by the farmhouse peeped gray out of its faithful grove; they saw the long lane with its convoy of walnut trees running from the road to the house; they smelled the wild rose and the breath of cool, damp willows in the creek's bed. And then in unison all the voices of the soil began a chant addressed to the soul of Robert Walmsley. Out of the tilted aisles of the dim wood they came hollowly; they chirped and buzzed from the parched grass; they trilled from the ripples of the creek ford; they floated up in clear Pan's pipe notes from the dimming meadows; the whippoorwills joined

149

in as they pursued midges in the upper air; slow-going cow-bells struck out a homely accompaniment—and this was what each one said: "You've found your way back at last, have you?"

The old voices of the soil spoke to him. Leaf and bud and blossom conversed with him in the old vocabulary of his careless youth—the inanimate things, the familiar stones and rails, the gates and furrows and roofs and turns of road had an eloquence, too, and a power in the transformation. The country had smiled and he had felt the breath of it, and his heart was drawn as if in a moment back to his old love. The city was far away.

This rural atavism, then, seized Robert Walmsley and possessed him. A queer thing he noticed in connection with it was that Alicia, sitting at his side, suddenly seemed to him a stranger. She did not belong to this recurrent phase. Never before had she seemed so remote, so colorless and high—so intangible and unreal. And yet he had never admired her more than when she sat there by him in the rickety spring wagon, chiming no more with his mood and with her environment than the Matterhorn chimes with a peasant's cabbage garden.

That night when the greetings and the supper were over, the entire family, including Buff, the yellow dog, bestrewed itself upon the front porch.

Alicia, not haughty but silent, sat in the shadow dressed in an exquisite pale-gray tea gown. Robert's mother discoursed to her happily concerning marmalade and lumbago. Tom sat on the top step; Sisters Millie and Pam on the lowest step to catch the lightning bugs. Mother had the willow rocker. Father sat in the big armchair with one of its arms gone. Buff sprawled in the middle of the porch in everybody's way. The twilight pixes and pucks stole forth unseen and plunged other poignant shafts of memory into the heart of Robert. A rural madness entered his soul. The city was far away.

Father sat without his pipe, writhing in his heavy boots, a sacrifice to rigid courtesy. Robert shouted: "No, you don't!" He fetched the pipe and lit it; he seized the old gentleman's boots and tore them off. The last one slipped suddenly, and Mr. Robert Walmsley, of Washington Square, tumbled off the porch backward with Buff on top of him, howling fearfully. Tom laughed sarcastically.

Robert tore off his coat and vest and hurled them into a lilac bush.

"Come out here, you landlubber," he cried to Tom, "and I'll put grass seed on your back. I think you called me a 'dude' a while ago. Come along and cut your capers."

Tom understood the invitation and accepted it

151

with delight. Three times they wrestled on the grass, "side holds," even as the giants of the mat. And twice was Tom forced to bite grass at the hands of the distinguished lawyer. Dishevelled, panting, each still boasting of his own prowess, they stumbled back to the porch. Millie cast a pert reflection upon the qualities of a city brother. In an instant Robert had secured a horrid katydid in his fingers and bore down upon her. Screaming wildly, she fled up the lane pursued by the avenging glass of form. A quarter of a mile and they returned, she full of apology to the victorious "dude." The rustic mania possessed him unabatedly.

"I can do up a cowpenful of you slow hayseeds," he proclaimed, vaingloriously. "Bring on your bull-dogs, your hired men, and your log-rollers."

He turned handsprings on the grass that prodded Tom to envious sarcasm. And then, with a whoop, he clattered to the rear and brought back Uncle Ike, a battered colored retainer of the family, with his banjo, and strewed sand on the porch and danced "Chicken in the Bread Tray" and did buck-and-wing wonders for half an hour longer. Incredibly wild and boisterous things he did. He sang, he told stories that set all but one shrieking, he played the yokel, the humorous clodhopper; he was mad,

mad with the revival of the old life in his blood.

He became so extravagant that once his mother sought gently to reprove him. Then Alicia moved as though she were about to speak, but she did not. Through it all she sat immovable, a slim, white spirit in the dusk that no man might question or read.

By and by she asked permission to ascend to her room, saying that she was tired. On her way she passed Robert. He was standing in the door, the figure of vulgar comedy, with ruffled hair, reddened face and unpardonable confusion of attire—no trace there of the immaculate Robert Walmsley, the courted clubman and ornament of select circles. He was doing a conjuring trick with some household utensils, and the family, now won over to him without exception, was beholding him with worshipful admiration.

As Alicia passed in Robert started suddenly. He had forgotten for the moment that she was present. Without a glance at him she went on upstairs.

After that the fun grew quiet. An hour passed in talk, and then Robert went up himself.

She was standing by the window when he entered their room. She was still clothed as when they were on the porch. Outside and crowding against

153

the window was a giant apple tree, full blossomed.

Robert sighed and went near the window. He was ready to meet his fate. A confessed vulgarian, he foresaw the verdict of justice in the shape of that still, whiteclad form. He knew the rigid lines that a Van Der Pool would draw. He was a peasant gambolling indecorously in the valley, and the pure, cold, white, unthawed summit of the Matterhorn could not but frown on him. He had been unmasked by his own actions. All the polish, the poise, the form that the city had given him had fallen from him like an ill-fitting mantle at the first breath of a country breeze. Dully he awaited the approaching condemnation.

"Robert," said the calm, cool voice of his judge, "I thought I married a gentleman."

Yes, it was coming. And yet, in the face of it, Robert Walmsley was eagerly regarding a certain branch of the apple tree upon which he used to climb out of that very window. He believed he could do it now. He wondered how many blossoms there were on the tree—ten millions? But here was someone speaking again:

"I thought I married a gentleman," the voice went on, "but——"

Why had she come and was standing so close by his side?

154

"But I find that I have married"—was this Alicia talking?—"something better—a man— Bob, dear, kiss me, won't you?"

The city was far away.

AFTER TWENTY YEARS

THE POLICEMAN on the beat moved up the avenue impressively. The impressiveness was habitual and not for show, for spectators were few. The time was barely 10 o'clock at night, but chilly gusts of wind with a taste of rain in them had well nigh depeopled the streets.

Trying doors as he went, twirling his club with many intricate and artful movements, turning now and then to cast his watchful eye adown the pacific thoroughfare, the officer, with his stalwart form and slight swagger, made a fine picture of a guardian of the peace. The vicinity was one that kept early hours. Now and then you might see the lights of a cigar store or of an all-night lunch counter; but the majority of the doors belonged to business places that had long since been closed.

When about midway of a certain block the policeman suddenly slowed his walk. In the doorway of a darkened hardware store a man leaned, with an unlighted cigar in his mouth. As the policeman walked up to him the man spoke up quickly.

"It's all right, officer," he said, reassuringly. "I'm just waiting for a friend. It's an appointment made twenty years ago. Sounds a little funny to you, doesn't it? Well, I'll explain if you'd like to make certain it's all straight. About that long ago there used to be a restaurant where this store stands— 'Big Joe' Brady's restaurant."

"Until five years ago," said the policeman. "It was torn down then."

The man in the doorway struck a match and lit his cigar. The light showed a pale, square-jawed face with keen eyes, and a little white scar near his right eyebrow. His scarfpin was a large diamond, oddly set.

"Twenty years ago to-night," said the man, "I dined here at 'Big Joe' Brady's with Jimmy Wells, my best chum, and the finest chap in the world. He and I were raised here in New York, just like two brothers, together. I was eighteen and Jimmy was twenty. The next morning I was to start for the West to make my fortune. You couldn't have dragged Jimmy out of New York; he thought it was the only place on earth. Well, we agreed that night that we would meet here again exactly twenty years from that date and time, no matter what our conditions might be or from what distance we might have to come. We figured that in twenty years each of us ought to have our destiny worked out and our fortunes made, whatever they were going to be."

"It sounds pretty interesting," said the policeman. "Rather a long time between meets, though, it seems to me. Haven't you heard from your friend since you left?"

"Well, yes, for a time we corresponded," said the other. "But after a year or two we lost track of each other. You see, the West is a pretty big proposition, and I kept hustling around over it pretty lively. But I know Jimmy will meet me here if he's alive, for he always was the truest, stanchest old chap in the world. He'll never forget. I came a thousand miles to stand in this door to-night, and it's worth it if my old partner turns up."

The waiting man pulled out a handsome watch, the lids of it set with small diamonds.

"Three minutes to ten," he announced. "It was exactly ten o'clock when we parted here at the restaurant door."

"Did pretty well out West, didn't you?" asked the policeman.

"You bet! I hope Jimmy has done half as well. He was a kind of plodder, though, good fellow as he was. I've had to compete with some of the sharpest wits going to get my pile. A man gets in a groove in New York. It takes the West to put a razor-edge on him."

The policeman twirled his club and took a step or two.

"I'll be on my way. Hope your friend comes around all right. Going to call time on him sharp?"

"I should say not!" said the other. "I'll give him half an hour at least. If Jimmy is alive on earth he'll be here by that time. So long, officer."

"Good-night, sir," said the policeman, passing on along his beat, trying doors as he went.

There was now a fine, cold drizzle falling, and the wind had risen from its uncertain puffs into a steady blow. The few foot passengers astir in that quarter hurried dismally and silently along with coat collars turned high and pocketed hands. And in the door of the hardware store the man who had come a thousand miles to fill an appointment, uncertain almost to absurdity, with the friend of his youth, smoked his cigar and waited.

About twenty minutes he waited, and then a

tall man in a long overcoat, with collar turned up to his ears, hurried across from the opposite side of the street. He went directly to the waiting man.

"Is that you, Bob?" he asked, doubtfully.

"Is that you, Jimmy Wells?" cried the man in the door.

"Bless my heart!" exclaimed the new arrival, grasping both the other's hands with his own. "It's Bob, sure as fate. I was certain I'd find you here if you were still in existence. Well, well, well!— twenty years is a long time. The old restaurant's gone, Bob; I wish it had lasted, so we could have had another dinner there. How has the West treated you, old man?"

"Bully; it has given me everything I asked it for. You've changed lots, Jimmy. I never thought you were so tall by two or three inches."

"Oh, I grew a bit after I was twenty."

"Doing well in New York, Jimmy?"

"Moderately. I have a position in one of the city departments. Come on, Bob; we'll go around to a place I know of, and have a good long talk about old times."

The two men started up the street, arm in arm. The man from the West, his egotism enlarged by success, was beginning to outline the history of his career. The other, submerged in his overcoat, listened with interest.

At the corner stood a drug store, brilliant with electric lights. When they came into this glare each of them turned simultaneously to gaze upon the other's face.

The man from the West stopped suddenly and released his arm.

"You're not Jimmy Wells," he snapped. "Twenty years is a long time, but not long enough to change a man's nose from a Roman to a pug."

"It sometimes changes a good man into a bad one," said the tall man. "You've been under arrest for ten minutes, 'Silky' Bob. Chicago thinks you may have dropped over our way and wires us she wants to have a chat with you. Going quietly, are you? That's sensible. Now, before we go to the station here's a note I was asked to hand you. You may read it here at the window. It's from Patrolman Wells."

The man from the West unfolded the little piece of paper handed him. His hand was steady when he began to read, but it trembled a little by the time he had finished. The note was rather short.

Bob: I was at the appointed place on time.

When you struck the match to light your cigar I saw it was the face of the man wanted in Chicago. Somehow I couldn't do it myself, so I went around and got a plain clothes man to do the job.

JIMMY.

A RETRIEVED REFORMATION

A GUARD CAME to the prison shoe-shop, where Jimmy Valentine was assiduously stitching uppers, and escorted him to the front office. There the warden handed Jimmy his pardon, which had been signed that morning by the governor. Jimmy took it in a tired kind of way. He had served nearly ten months of a four-year sentence. He had expected to stay only about three months, at the longest. When a man with as many friends on the outside as Jimmy Valentine had is received in the "stir" it is hardly worth while to cut his hair.

"Now, Valentine," said the warden, "you'll go out in the morning. Brace up, and make a man of yourself. You're not a bad fellow at heart. Stop cracking safes, and live straight."

"Me?" said Jimmy, in surprise. "Why, I never cracked a safe in my life."

"Oh, no," laughed the warden. "Of course not. Let's see, now. How was it you happened to get sent up on that Springfield job? Was it because you wouldn't prove an alibi for fear of compromising somebody in extremely high-toned society? Or was it simply a case of a mean old jury that had it in for you? It's always one or the other with you innocent victims."

"Me?" said Jimmy, still blankly virtuous. "Why, warden, I never was in Springfield in my life!"

"Take him back, Cronin," smiled the warden, "and fix him up with outgoing clothes. Unlock him at seven in the morning, and let him come to the bull-pen. Better think over my advice, Valentine."

At a quarter past seven on the next morning Jimmy stood in the warden's outer office. He had on a suit of the villainously fitting, ready-made clothes and a pair of the stiff, squeaky shoes that the state furnishes to its discharged compulsory guests.

The clerk handed him a railroad ticket and the five-dollar bill with which the law expected him to rehabilitate himself into good citizenship and prosperity. The warden gave him a cigar, and shook hands. Valentine, 9762, was chronicled on the books "Pardoned by Governor," and Mr. James Valentine walked out into the sunshine.

Disregarding the song of the birds, the waving green trees, and the smell of the flowers, Jimmy headed straight for a restaurant. There he tasted the first sweet joys of liberty in the shape of a broiled chicken and a bottle of white wine—followed by a cigar a grade better than the one the warden had given him. From there he proceeded leisurely to the depot. He tossed a quarter into the hat of a blind man sitting by the door, and boarded his train. Three hours set him down in a little town near the state line. He went to the café of one Mike Dolan and shook hands with Mike, who was alone behind the bar.

"Sorry we couldn't make it sooner, Jimmy, me boy," said Mike. "But we had that protest from Springfield to buck against, and the governor nearly balked. Feeling all right?"

"Fine," said Jimmy. "Got my key?"

He got his key and went upstairs, unlocking the door of a room at the rear. Everything was just as he had left it. There on the floor was still Ben Price's collar-button that had been torn from that eminent detective's shirt-band when they had overpowered Jimmy to arrest him.

Pulling out from the wall a folding-bed, Jimmy slid back a panel in the wall and dragged out a dust-covered suit-case. He opened this and gazed fondly at the finest set of burglar's tools in the East. It was a complete set, made of specially tempered steel, the latest designs in drills, punches, braces and bits, jimmies, clamps, and augers, with two or three novelties invented by Jimmy himself, in which he took pride. Over nine hundred dollars they had cost him to have made at——, a place where they make such things for the profession.

In half an hour Jimmy went downstairs and through the café. He was now dressed in tasteful and well-fitting clothes, and carried his dusted and cleaned suitcase in his hand.

"Got anything on?" asked Mike Dolan, genially.

"Me?" said Jimmy, in a puzzled tone. "I don't understand. I'm representing the New York Amalgamated Short Snap Biscuit Cracker and Frazzled Wheat Company."

This statement delighted Mike to such an extent that Jimmy had to take a seltzer-and-milk on the spot. He never touched "hard" drinks.

A week after the release of Valentine, 9762, there was a neat job of safe-burglary done in Richmond, Indiana, with no clue to the author. A scant eight hundred dollars was all that was secured. Two weeks after that a patented, improved, burglar-proof safe in Logansport was opened like a

166

cheese to the tune of fifteen hundred dollars, currency; securities and silver untouched. That began to interest the rogue-catchers. Then an old-fashioned bank-safe in Jefferson City became active and threw out of its crater an eruption of banknotes amounting to five thousand dollars. The loses were now high enough to bring the matter up into Ben Price's class of work. By comparing notes, a remarkable similarity in the methods of the burglaries was noticed. Ben Price investigated the scenes of the robberies, and was heard to remark:

"That's Dandy Jim Valentine's autograph. He's resumed business. Look at that combination knob —jerked out as easy as pulling up a radish in wet weather. He's got the only clamps that can do it. And look how clean those tumblers were punched out! Jimmy never has to drill but one hole. Yes, I guess I want Mr. Valentine. He'll do his bit next time without any short-time or clemency foolishness."

Ben Price knew Jimmy's habits. He had learned them while working up the Springfield case. Long jumps, quick get-aways, no confederates, and a taste for good society—these ways had helped Mr. Valentine to become noted as a successful dodger of retribution. It was given out that Ben Price had taken up the trail of the elusive cracksman, and other people with burglar-proof safes felt more at ease.

One afternoon Jimmy Valentine and his suit-case climbed out of the mailhack in Elmore, a little town five miles off the railroad down in the black-jack country of Arkansas. Jimmy, looking like an athletic young senior just home from college, went down the board sidewalk toward the hotel.

A young lady crossed the street, passed him at the corner and entered a door over which was the sign "The Elmore Bank." Jimmy Valentine looked into her eyes, forgot what he was, and became another man. She lowered her eyes and colored slightly. Young men of Jimmy's style and looks were scarce in Elmore.

Jimmy collared a boy that was loafing on the steps of the bank as if he were one of the stockholders, and began to ask him questions about the town, feeding him dimes at intervals. By and by the young lady came out, looking royally unconscious of the young man with the suitcase, and went her way.

"Isn't that young lady Miss Polly Simpson?" asked Jimmy, with specious guile.

"Naw," said the boy. "She's Annabel Adams. Her pa owns this bank. What'd you come to Elmore for? Is that a gold watch-chain? I'm going to get a bulldog. Got any more dimes?"

Jimmy went to the Planters' Hotel, registered as Ralph D. Spencer, and engaged a room. He leaned on the desk and declared his platform to the clerk. He said he had come to Elmore to look for a location to go into business. How was the shoe business, now, in the town? He had thought of the shoe business. Was there an opening?

The clerk was impressed by the clothes and manner of Jimmy. He, himself, was something of a pattern of fashion to the thinly gilded youth of Elmore, but he now perceived his shortcomings. While trying to figure out Jimmy's manner of tying his four-in-hand he cordially gave information.

Yes, there ought to be a good opening in the shoe line. There wasn't an exclusive shoe-store in the place. The dry-goods and general stores handled them. Business in all lines was fairly good. Hoped Mr. Spencer would decide to locate in Elmore. He would find it a pleasant town to live in, and the people very sociable.

Mr. Spencer thought he would stop over in the town a few days and look over the situation. No, the clerk needn't call the boy. He would carry up his suitcase, himself; it was rather heavy.

Mr. Ralph Spencer, the phœnix that arose from

Jimmy Valentine's ashes—ashes left by the flame of a sudden and alterative attack of love—remained in Elmore, and prospered. He opened a shoe-store and secured a good run of trade.

Socially he was also a success, and made many friends. And he accomplished the wish of his heart. He met Miss Annabel Adams, and became more and more captivated by her charms.

At the end of a year the situation of Mr. Ralph Spencer was this: he had won the respect of the community, his shoe-store was flourishing, and he and Annabel were engaged to be married in two weeks. Mr. Adams, the typical, plodding, country banker, approved of Spencer. Annabel's pride in him almost equalled her affection. He was as much at home in the family of Mr. Adams and that of Annabel's married sister as if he were already a member.

One day Jimmy sat down in his room and wrote this letter, which he mailed to the safe address of one of his old friends in St. Louis:

DEAR OLD PAL:

I want you to be at Sullivan's place, in Little Rock, next Wednesday night, at nine o'clock. I want you to wind up some little matters for me.

And, also, I want to make you a present of my kit of tools. I know you'll be glad to get them—you couldn't duplicate the lot for a thousand dollars. Say, Billy, I've quit the old business—a year ago. I've got a nice store. I'm making an honest living, and I'm going to marry the finest girl on earth two weeks from now. It's the only life, Billy—the straight one. I wouldn't touch a dollar of another man's money now for a million. After I get married I'm going to sell out and go West, where there won't be so much danger of having old scores brought up against me. I tell you, Billy, she's an angel. She believes in me; and I wouldn't do another crooked thing for the whole world. Be sure to be at Sully's, for I must see you. I'll bring along the tools with me.

Your old friend,
JIMMY.

On the Monday night after Jimmy wrote this letter, Ben Price jogged unobtrusively into Elmore in a livery buggy. He lounged about town in his quiet way until he found out what he wanted to know. From the drug-store across the street from Spencer's shoe-store he got a good look at Ralph D. Spencer.

"Going to marry the banker's daughter are you, Jimmy?" said Ben to himself, softly. "Well, I don't know!"

The next morning Jimmy took breakfast at the Adamses. He was going to Little Rock that day to order his wedding-suit and buy something nice for Annabel. That would be the first time he had left town since he came to Elmore. It had been more than a year now since those last professional "jobs," and he thought he could safely venture out.

After breakfast quite a family party went down together—Mr. Adams, Annabel, Jimmy, and Annabel's married sister with her two little girls, aged five and nine. They came by the hotel where Jimmy still boarded, and he ran up to his room and brought along his suitcase. Then they went on to the bank. There stood Jimmy's horse and buggy and Dolph Gibson, who was going to drive him over to the railroad station.

All went inside the high, carved oak railings into the banking-room—Jimmy included, for Mr. Adam's future son-in-law was welcome anywhere. The clerks were pleased to be greeted by the good-looking, agreeable young man who was going to marry Miss Annabel. Jimmy set his suit-case down. Annabel, whose heart was bubbling with happiness and lively youth, put on Jimmy's hat and picked up the suit-case. "Wouldn't I make a nice drum-mer?" said Annabel. "My! Ralph, how heavy it is. Feels like it was full of gold bricks."

"Lot of nickel-plated shoe-horns in there," said Jimmy, coolly, "that I'm going to return. Thought I'd save express charges by taking them up. I'm getting awfully economical."

The Elmore Bank had just put in a new safe and vault. Mr. Adams was very proud of it, and insisted on an inspection by every one. The vault was a small one, but it had a new patented door. It fastened with three solid steel bolts thrown simul-taneously with a single handle, and had a time-lock. Mr. Adams beamingly explained its workings to Mr. Spencer, who showed a courteous but not too intelligent interest. The two children, May and Agatha, were delighted by the shining metal and funny clock and knobs.

While they were thus engaged Ben Price saun-tered in and leaned on his elbow, looking casually inside between the railings. He told the teller that he didn't want anything; he was just waiting for a man he knew.

Suddenly there was a scream or two from the women, and a commotion. Unperceived by the elders, May, the nine-year-old girl, in a spirit of play, had shut Agatha in the vault. She had then shot the bolts and turned the knob of the combination as she had seen Mr. Adams do.

The old banker sprang to the handle and tugged at it for a moment. "The door can't be opened," he groaned. "The clock hasn't been wound nor the combination set."

Agatha's mother screamed again, hysterically.

"Hush!" said Mr. Adams, raising his trembling hand. "All be quiet for a moment. Agatha!" he called as loudly as he could. "Listen to me." During the following silence they could just hear the faint sound of the child wildly shrieking in the dark vault in a panic of terror.

"My precious darling!" wailed the mother. "She will die of fright! Open the door! Oh, break it open! Can't you men do something?"

"There isn't a man nearer than Little Rock who can open that door," said Mr. Adams, in a shaky voice. "My God! Spencer, what shall we do? That child—she can't stand it long in there. There isn't enough air, and, besides, she'll go into convulsions from fright."

Agatha's mother, frantic now, beat the door of the vault with her hands. Somebody wildly suggested dynamite. Annabel turned to Jimmy, her large eyes full of anguish, but not yet despairing.

To a woman nothing seems quite impossible to the powers of the man she worships.

"Can't you do something, Ralph—*try,* won't you?"

He looked at her with a queer, soft smile on his lips and in his keen eyes.

"Annabel," he said, "give me that rose you are wearing, will you?"

Hardly believing that she heard him aright, she unpinned the bud from the bosom of her dress, and placed it in his hand. Jimmy stuffed it into his vest-pocket, threw off his coat and pulled up his shirt-sleeves. With that act Ralph D. Spencer passed away and Jimmy Valentine took his place.

"Get way from the door, all of you," he commanded, shortly.

He set his suit-case on the table, and opened it out flat. From that time on he seemed to be unconscious of the presence of any one else. He laid out the shining, queer implements swiftly and orderly, whistling softly to himself as he always did when at work. In a deep silence and immovable, the others watched him as if under a spell.

In a minute Jimmy's pet drill was biting smoothly into the steel door. In ten minutes—breaking his own burglarious record—he threw back the bolts and opened the door.

Agatha, almost collapsed, but safe, was gathered into her mother's arms.

Jimmy Valentine put on his coat, and walked outside the railings toward the front door. As he went he thought he heard a far-away voice that he once knew call "Ralph!" But he never hesitated.

At the door a big man stood somewhat in his way.

"Hello, Ben!" said Jimmy, still with his strange smile. "Got around at last, have you? Well, let's go. I don't know that it makes much difference, now."

And then Ben Price acted rather strangely.

"Guess you're mistaken, Mr. Spencer," he said. "Don't believe I recognize you. Your buggy's waiting for you, ain't it?"

And Ben Price turned and strolled down the street.

FRIENDS IN SAN ROSARIO

THE WEST-BOUND stopped at San Rosario on time
at 8:20 A.M. A man with a thick black-leather wallet under his arm left the train and walked rapidly
up the main street of the town. There were other
passengers who also got off at San Rosario, but
they either slouched limberly over to the railroad
eating-house or the Silver Dollar saloon, or joined
the groups of idlers about the station.

Indecision had no part in the movements of the
man with the wallet. He was short in stature, but
strongly built, with very light, closely trimmed hair,
smooth, determined face, and aggressive, gold-rim-
med nose glasses. He was well dressed in the pre-
vailing Eastern style. His air denoted a quiet but
conscious reserve force, if not actual authority.

After walking a distance of three squares he
came to the center of the town's business area. Here

another street of importance crossed the main one, forming the hub of San Rosario's life and commerce. Upon one corner stood the post-office. Upon another Rubensky's Clothing Emporium. The other two diagonally opposing corners were occupied by the town's two banks, the First National and the Stockmen's National. Into the First National Bank of San Rosario the newcomer walked, never slowing his brisk step until he stood at the cashier's window. The bank opened for business at nine, and the working force was already assembled, each member preparing his department for the day's business. The cashier was examining the mail when he noticed the stranger standing at his window.

"Bank doesn't open 'til nine," he remarked, curtly, but without feeling. He had had to make that statement so often to early birds since San Rosario adopted city banking hours.

"I am well aware of that," said the other man, in cool, brittle tones. "Will you kindly receive my card?"

J. F. C. NETTLEWICK
National Bank Examiner

"Oh—er—will you walk around inside, Mr.—

178

er—Nettlewick. Your first visit—didn't know your business, of course. Walk right around, please."

The examiner was quickly inside the sacred precincts of the bank, where he was ponderously introduced to each employee in turn by Mr. Edlinger, the cashier—a middle-aged gentleman of deliberation, discretion, and method.

"I was kind of expecting Sam Turner round again, pretty soon," said Mr. Edlinger. "Sam's been examining us now for about four years. I guess you'll find us all right, though, considering the tightness in business. Not overly much money on hand, but able to stand the storms, sir, stand the storms."

"Mr. Turner and I have been ordered by the Comptroller to exchange districts," said the examiner, in his decisive, formal tones. "He is covering my old territory in southern Illinois and Indiana. I will take the cash first, please."

Perry Dorsey, the teller, was already arranging his cash on the counter for the examiner's inspection. He know it was right to a cent, and he had nothing to fear, but he was nervous and flustered. So was every man in the bank. There was something so icy and swift, so impersonal and uncompromising about this man that his very presence seemed an accusation. He looked to be a man who would never make nor overlook an error.

Mr. Nettlewick first seized the currency, and with a rapid, almost juggling motion, counted it by packages. Then he spun the sponge cup toward him and verified the count by bills. His thin, white fingers flew like some expert musician's upon the keys of a piano. He dumped the gold upon the counter with a crash, and the coins whined and sang as they skimmed across the marble slab from the tips of his nimble digits. The air was full of fractional currency when he came to the halves and quarters. He counted the last nickel and dime. He had the scales brought, and he weighed every sack of silver in the vault. He questioned Dorsey concerning each of the cash memoranda—certain checks, charge slips, etc., carried over from the previous day's work—with unimpeachable courtesy, yet with something so mysteriously momentous in his frigid manner, that the teller was reduced to pink cheeks and a stammering tongue.

This newly imported examiner was so different from Sam Turner. It had been Sam's way to enter the bank with a shout, pass the cigars, and tell the latest stories he had picked up on his rounds. His customary greeting to Dorsey had been, "Hello,

Perry! Haven't skipped out with the boodle yet, I see." Turner's way of counting the cash had been different, too. He would finger the packages of bills in a tired kind of way, and then go into the vault and kick over a few sacks of silver, and the thing was done. Halves and quarters and dimes? Not for Sam Turner. "No chicken feed for me," he would say when they were set before him. "I'm not in the agricultural department." But, then, Turner was a Texan, and old friend of the bank's president, and had known Dorsey since he was a baby.

While the examiner was counting the cash, Major Thomas B. Kingman—known to every one as "Major Tom"—the president of the First National, drove up to the side door with his old dun horse and buggy, and came inside. He saw the examiner busy with the money, and, going into the little "pony corral," as he called it, in which his desk was railed off, he began to look over his letters.

Earlier, a little incident had occurred that even the sharp eyes of the examiner had failed to notice. When he had begun his work at the cash counter, Mr. Edlinger had winked significantly at Roy Wilson, the youthful bank messenger, and nodded his head slightly toward the front door. Roy understood, got his hat and walked leisurely out, with his collector's book under his arm. Once outside, he made a beeline for the Stockmen's National. That bank was also getting ready to open. No customers had, as yet, presented themselves.

"Say, you people!" cried Roy, with the familiarity of youth and long acquaintance, "you want to get a move on you. There's a new bank examiner over at the First, and he's a stem-winder. He's counting nickels on Perry, and he's got the whole outfit bluffed. Mr. Edlinger gave me the tip to let you know."

Mr. Buckley, president of the Stockmen's National—a stout, elderly man, looking like a farmer dressed for Sunday—heard Roy from his private office at the rear and called him.

"Has Major Kingman come down to the bank yet?" he asked of the boy.

"Yes, sir, he was just driving up as I left," said Roy.

"I want you to take him a note. Put it into his own hands as soon as you get back."

Mr. Buckley sat down and began to write.

Roy returned and handed to Major Kingman the envelope containing the note. The major read it, folded it, and slipped it into his vest pocket. He leaned back in his chair for a few moments as if he were meditating deeply, and then rose and went into the vault. He came out with the bulky, old-fashioned leather note case stamped on the back in gilt letters, "Bills Discounted." In this were the notes due the bank with their attached securities, and the major, in his rough way, dumped the lot upon his desk and began to sort them over.

By this time Nettlewick had finished his count of the cash. His pencil fluttered like a swallow over the sheet of paper on which he had set his figures. He opened his black wallet, which seemed to be also a kind of secret memorandum book, made a few rapid figures in it, wheeled and transfixed Dorsey with the glare of his spectacles. That look seemed to say: "You're safe this time, but——"

"Cash all correct," snapped the examiner. He made a dash for the individual bookkeeper, and, for a few minutes there was a fluttering of ledger leaves and a sailing of balance sheets through the air.

"How often do you balance your pass-books?" he demanded, suddenly.

"Er—once a month," faltered the individual bookkeeper, wondering how many years they would give him.

"All right," said the examiner, turning and

charging upon the general bookkeeper, who had the statements of his foreign banks and their reconcilement memoranda ready. Everything there was found to be all right. Then the stub book of the certificates of deposit. Flutter—flutter—zip—zip—check! All right. List of over-drafts, please. Thanks. H'm-m. Unsigned bills of the bank, next. All right.

Then came the cashier's turn, and easy-going Mr. Edlinger rubbed his nose and polished his glasses nervously under the quick fire of questions concerning the circulation, undivided profits, bank real estate, and stock ownership.

Presently Nettlewick was aware of a big man towering above him at his elbow—a man sixty years of age, rugged and hale, with a rough, grizzled beard, a mass of gray hair, and a pair of penetrating blue eyes that confronted the formidable glasses of the examiner without a flicker.

"Er—Major Kingman, our president—er—Mr. Nettlewick," said the cashier.

Two men of very different types shook hands. One was a finished product of the world of straight lines, conventional methods, and formal affairs. The other was something freer, wider, and nearer to nature. Tom Kingman had not been cut to any pattern. He had been mule-driver, cowboy, ranger, soldier, sheriff, prospector and cattleman. Now, when he was bank president, his old comrades from the prairies, of the saddle, tent, and trail, found no change in him. He had made his fortune when Texas cattle were at the high tide of value, and had organized the First National Bank of San Rosario. In spite of his largeness of heart and sometimes unwise generosity toward his old friends, the bank had prospered, for Major Tom Kingman knew men as well as he knew cattle. Of late years the cattle business had known a depression, and the major's bank was one of the few whose losses had not been great.

"And now," said the examiner, briskly, pulling out his watch, "the last thing is the loans. We will take them up now, if you please."

He had gone through the First National at almost record-breaking speed—but thoroughly, as he did everything. The running order to the bank was smooth and clean, and that had facilitated his work. There was but one other bank in the town. He received from the Government a fee of twenty-five dollars for each bank that he examined. He should be able to go over those loans and discounts in half an hour. If so, he could examine the other bank immediately afterward, and catch the 11:45, the only other train that day in the direction he was working. Otherwise, he would have to spend the night and Sunday in this uninteresting Western town. That was why Mr. Nettlewick was rushing matters.

"Come with me, sir," said Major Kingman, in his deep voice, that united the Southern drawl with the rhythmic twang of the West; "We will go over them together. Nobody in the bank knows those notes as I do. Some of 'em are a little wobbly on their legs, and some are mavericks without extra many brands on their backs, but they'll 'most all pay out at the round-up."

The two sat down at the president's desk. First, the examiner went through the notes at lightning speed, and added up their total, finding it to agree with the amount of loans carried on the book of daily balances. Next, he took up the larger loans, inquiring scrupulously into the condition of their endorsers or securities. The new examiner's mind seemed to course and turn and make unexpected dashes hither and thither like a bloodhound seeking a trail. Finally he pushed aside all the notes except a few, which he arranged in a neat pile before him, and began a dry, formal little speech.

"I find, sir, the condition of your bank to be very good, considering the poor crops and the depression in the cattle interests of your state. The clerical work seems to be done accurately and punctually. Your past-due paper is moderate in amount, and promises only a small loss. I would recommend the calling in of your large loans, and the making of only sixty and ninety day or call loans until general business revives. And now, there is one thing more, and I will have finished with the bank. Here are six notes aggregating something like $40,000. They are secured, according to their faces, by various stocks, bonds, shares, etc., to the value of $70,000. Those securities are missing from the notes to which they should be attached. I suppose you have them in the safe or vault. You will permit me to examine them."

Major Tom's light-blue eyes turned unflinchingly toward the examiner.

"No, sir," he said, in a low but steady tone; "those securities are neither in the safe nor the vault. I have taken them. You may hold me personally responsible for their absence."

Nettlewick left a slight thrill. He had not expected this. He had struck a momentous trail when the hunt was drawing to a close.

"Ah!" said the examiner. He waited a moment, and then continued: "May I ask you to explain more definitely?"

187

"The securities were taken by me," repeated the major. "It was not for my own use, but to save an old friend in trouble. Come in here, sir, and we'll talk it over."

He led the examiner into the bank's private office at the rear, and closed the door. There was a desk, and a table, and half-a-dozen leather-covered chairs. On the wall was the mounted head of a Texas steer with horns five feet from tip to tip. Opposite hung the major's old cavalry saber that he had carried at Shiloh and Fort Pillow.

Placing a chair for Nettlewick, the major seated himself by the window, from which he could see the post-office and the carved limestone front of the Stockman's National. He did not speak at once, and Nettlewick felt, perhaps, that the ice should be broken by something so near its own temperature as the voice of official warning.

"Your statement," he began, "since you have failed to modify it, amounts, as you must know, to a very serious thing. You are aware, also, of what my duty must compel me to do. I shall have to go before the United States Commissioner and make——"

"I know, I know," said Major Tom, with a wave of his hand. "You don't suppose I'd run a bank without being posted on national banking laws and the revised statutes! Do your duty. I'm not asking any favors. But I spoke of my friend. I did want you to hear me tell you about Bob."

Nettlewick settled himself in his chair. There would be no leaving San Rosario for him that day. He would have to telegraph to the Comptroller of the Currency; he would have to swear out a warrant before the United States Commissioner for the arrest of Major Kingman; perhaps he would be ordered to close the bank on account of the loss of the securities. It was not the first crime the examiner had unearthed. Once or twice the terrible upheaval of human emotions that his investigations had loosed had almost caused a ripple in his official calm. He had seen bank men kneel and plead and cry like women for a chance—an hour's time—the overlooking of a single error. One cashier had shot himself at his desk before him. None of them had taken it with the dignity and coolness of this stern old Westerner. Nettlewick felt that he owed it to him at least to listen if he wished to talk. With his elbow on the arm of his chair, and his square chin resting upon the fingers of his right hand, the bank examiner waited to hear the confession of the president of the First National Bank of San Rosario.

"When a man's your friend," began Major Tom, somewhat didactically, "for forty years, and tried by water, fire, earth, and cyclones, when you can do him a little favor you feel like doing it."

("Embezzle for him $70,000 worth of securities," thought the examiner.)

"We were cowboys together, Bob and I," continued the major, speaking slowly, and deliberately, and musingly, as if his thoughts were rather with the past than the critical present, "and we prospected together for gold and silver over Arizona, New Mexico, and a good part of California. We were both in the war of 'sixty-one, but in different commands. We've fought Indians and horse thieves side by side; we've starved for weeks in a cabin in the Arizona mountains, buried twenty feet deep in snow; we've ridden herd together when the wind blew so hard the lightning couldn't strike—well, Bob and I have been through some rough spells since the first time we met in the branding camp of the old Anchor-Bar ranch. And during that time we've found it necessary more than once to help each other out of tight places. In those days it was expected of a man to stick to his friend, and he didn't ask any credit for it. Probably next day you'd need him to get at your back and help stand off a band of Apaches, or put a tourniquet on your leg above a rattlesnake bite and ride for whisky. So, after all, it was give and take, and if you didn't stand square with your pardner, why, you might be shy one when you needed him. But Bob was a man who was willing to go further than that. He never played a limit.

"Twenty years ago I was sheriff of this county and I made Bob my chief deputy. That was before the boom in cattle when we both made our stake. I was sheriff and collector, and it was a big thing for me then, I was married, and we had a boy and a girl—a four and a six year old. There was a comfortable house next to the courthouse, furnished by the county, rent free, and I was saving some money. Bob did most of the office work. Both of us had seen rough times and plenty of rustling and danger, and I tell you it was great to hear the rain and the sleet dashing against the windows of nights, and be warm and safe and comfortable, and know you could get up in the morning and be shaved and have folks call you 'mister.' And then, I had the finest wife and kids that ever struck the range, and my old friend with me enjoying the first fruits of prosperity and white shirts, and I guess I was happy. Yes, I was happy about that time."

The major sighed and glanced casually out of the window. The bank examiner changed his position, and leaned his chin upon his other hand.

"One winter," continued the major, "the money

for the county taxes came pouring in so fast that I didn't have time to take the stuff to the bank for a week. I just shoved the checks into a cigar box and the money into a sack, and locked them in the big safe that belonged in the sheriff's office.

"I had been overworked that week, and was about sick, anyway. My nerves were out of order, and my sleep at night didn't seem to rest me. The doctor had some scientific name for it, and I was taking medicine. And so, added to the rest, I went to bed at night with that money on my mind. Not that there was much need of being worried, for the safe was a good one, and nobody but Bob and I know the combination. On Friday night there was about $6,500 in cash in the bag. On Saturday morning I went to the office as usual. The safe was locked, and Bob was writing at his desk. I opened the safe, and the money was gone. I called Bob, and roused everybody in the courthouse to announce the robbery. It struck me that Bob took it pretty quiet, considering how much it reflected upon him and me.

"Two days went by and we never got a clew. It couldn't have been burglars, for the safe had been opened by the combination in the proper way. People must have begun to talk, for one afternoon in comes Alice—that's my wife— and the boy and

192

girl, and Alice stamps her foot, and her eyes flash, and she cries out, 'The lying wretches—Tom, Tom!' and I catch her in a faint, and bring her 'round little by little, and she lays her head down and cries and cries for the first time since she took Tom Kingman's name and fortunes. And Jack and Zilla—the youngsters—they were always wild as tigers cubs to rush at Bob and climb all over him whenever they were allowed to come to the court-house—they stood and kicked their little shoes, and herded together like scared partridges. They were having their first trip down into the shadows of life. Bob was working at his desk, and he got up and went out without a word. The grand jury was in session then, and the next morning Bob went before them and confessed that he stole the money. He said he lost it in a poker game. In fifteen minutes they had found a true bill and sent me the warrant to arrest the man with whom I'd been closer than a thousand brothers for many a year.

"I did it, and then I said to Bob, pointing: 'There's my house, and here's my office, and up there's Maine, and out that way is California, and over there is Florida—and that's your range 'til court meets. You're in my charge, and I take the responsibility. You be here when you're wanted.'

" 'Thanks, Tom,' he said, kind of carelessly; 'I

was sort of hoping you wouldn't lock me up. Court meets next Monday, so, if you don't object, I'll just loaf around the office until then. I've got one favor to ask, if it isn't too much. If you'd let the kids come out in the yard once in a while and have a romp I'd like it.'

"Why not?' I answered him. 'They're welcome, and so are you. And come to my house the same as ever.' You see, Mr. Nettlewick, you can't make a friend of a thief, but neither can you make a thief of a friend, all at once."

The examiner made no answer. At that moment was heard the shrill whistle of a locomotive pulling into the depot. That was the train on the little, narrow-gauge road that struck into San Rosario from the south. The major cocked his ear and listened for a moment, and looked at his watch. The narrow-gauge was in on time—10:35. The major continued:

"So Bob hung around the office, reading the papers and smoking. I put another deputy to work in his place, and, after a while, the first excitement of the case wore off.

"One day when we were alone in the office Bob came over to where I was sitting. He was looking sort of grim and blue—the same look he used to get when he'd been up watching for Indians all night or herd-riding.

" 'Tom,' says he, 'it's harder than standing off redskins; it's harder than lying in the lava desert forty miles from water; but I'm going to stick it out to the end. You know that's been my style. But if you'd tip me the smallest kind of a sign—if you'd just say, "Bob I understand," why, it would make it lots easier.'

"I was surprised. 'I don't know what you mean, Bob,' I said. 'Of course, you know that I'd do anything under the sun to help you that I could. But you've got me guessing.'

" 'All right, Tom,' was all he said, and he went back to his newspaper and lit another cigar.

"It was the night before the court met when I found out what he meant. I went to bed that night with the same old, light-headed, nervous feeling come back upon me. I dropped off to sleep about midnight. When I woke I was standing half dressed in one of the courthouse corridors. Bob was holding one of my arms, our family doctor the other, and Alice was shaking me and half crying. She had sent for the doctor without my knowing it, and when he came they had found me out of bed and missing, and had begun a search.

195

" 'Sleep-walking,' said the doctor.

"All of us went back to the house, and the doctor told us some remarkable stories about the strange things people had done while in that condition. I was feeling rather chilly after my trip out, and, as my wife was out of the room at the time, I pulled open the door of an old wardrobe that stood in the room and dragged out a big quilt I had seen in there. With it tumbled out the bag of money for which Bob was to be tried—and convicted—in the morning.

" 'How the jumping rattlesnakes did that get there?' I yelled, and all hands must have seen how surprised I was. Bob knew in a flash.

" 'You darned old snoozer,' he said, with the old-time look on his face, 'I saw you put it there. I watched you open the safe and take it out, and I followed you. I looked through the window and saw you hide it in that wardrobe.'

" 'Then, you blankety-blank, flop-eared, sheep-headed coyote, what did you say you took it for?'

" 'Because,' said Bob, simply, 'I didn't know you were asleep.'

"I saw him glance toward the door of the room where Jack and Zilla were, and I knew then what it meant to be a man's friend from Bob's point of view."

Major Tom paused, and again directed his glance out of the window. He saw someone in the Stockmen's National Bank reach and draw a yellow shade down the whole length of its plate-glass, big front window, although the position of the sun did not seem to warrant such a defensive movement against its rays.

Nettlewick sat up straight in his chair. He had listened patiently but without consuming interest, to the major's story. It had impressed him as irrelevant to the situation, and it could certainly have no effect upon the consequences. Those Western people, he thought, had an exaggerated sentimentality. They were not business-like. They needed to be protected from their friends. Evidently the major had concluded. And what he had said amounted to nothing.

"May I ask," said the examiner, "if you have anything further to say that bears directly upon the question of those abstracted securities?"

"Abstracted securities, sir!" Major Tom turned suddenly in his chair, his blue eyes flashing upon the examiner. "What do you mean, sir?"

He drew from his coat pocket a batch of folded papers held together by a rubber band, tossed them into Nettlewick's hands, and rose to his feet.

"You'll find those securities there, sir, every

stock, bond, and share of 'em. I took them from the notes while you were counting the cash. Examine and compare them for yourself."

The major led the way back into the banking room. The examiner, astounded, perplexed, nettled, at sea, followed. He felt that he had been made the victim of something that was not exactly a hoax, but that left him in the shoes of one who had been played upon, used, and then discarded, without even an inkling of the game. Perhaps, also, his official position had been irreverently juggled with. But there was nothing he could take hold of. An official report of the matter would be an absurdity. And, somehow, he felt that he would never know anything more about the matter than he did then.

Frigidly, mechanically, Nettlewick examined the securities, found them to tally with the notes, gathered his black wallet, and rose to depart.

"I will say," he protested, turning the indignant glare of his glasses upon Major Kingman, "that your statements—your misleading statements, which you have not condescended to explain—do not appear to be quite the thing, regarded either as business or humor. I do not understand such motives or actions."

Major Tom looked down at him serenely and not unkindly.

"Son," he said, "there are plenty of things in the chaparral, and on the prairies, and up the canons that you don't understand. But I want to thank you for listening to a garrulous old man's prosy story. We old Texans love to talk about our adventures and our old comrades, and the home folks have long ago learned to run when we begin with 'Once upon a time,' so we have to spin our yarns to the stranger within our gates."

The major smiled, but the examiner only bowed coldly, and abruptly quitted the bank. They saw him travel diagonally across the street in a straight line and enter the Stockmen's National Bank.

Major Tom sat down at his desk and drew from his vest pocket the note Roy had given him. He had read it once, but hurriedly, and now, with something like a twinkle in his eyes, he read it again. These were the words he read:

DEAR TOM:

I hear there's one of Uncle Sam's greyhound's going through you, and that means that we'll catch him inside of a couple of hours, maybe. Now, I want you to do something for me. We've got just $2,200 in the bank, and the law requires that we have $20,000. I let Ross and Fisher have $18,00 late yesterday afternoon to buy up that

Gibson bunch of cattle. They'll realize $40,000 in less than thirty days on the transaction, but that won't make my cash on hand look any prettier to that bank examiner. Now, I can't show him those notes, for they're just plain notes of hand without any security in sight, but you know very well that Pink Ross and Jim Fisher are two of the finest white men God ever made, and they'll do the square thing. You remember Jim Fisher—he was the one who shot that faro dealer in El Paso. I wired Sam Bradshaw's bank to send me $20,000, and it will get in on the narrow-gauge at 10:35. You can't let a bank examiner in to count $2,200 and close your doors. Tom, you hold that examiner. Hold him. Hold him if you have to rope him and sit on his head. Watch our front window after the narrow-gauge gets in, and when we've got the cash inside we'll pull down the shade for a signal. Don't turn him loose till then. I'm counting on you, Tom.

Your Old Pard,

BOB BUCKLEY,

Prest. Stockmen's National.

The major began to tear the note into small pieces and throw them into his waste basket. He gave a satisfied little chuckle as he did so.

"Confounded old reckless cowpuncher!" he growled, contentedly, "that pays him some on account for what he tried to do for me in the sheriff's office twenty years ago."

ONE DOLLAR'S WORTH

THE JUDGE of the United States court of the district lying along the Rio Grande border found the following letter one morning in his mail:

JUDGE:

When you sent me up for four years you made a talk. Among other hard things, you called me a rattlesnake. Maybe I am one—anyhow, you hear me rattling now. One year after I got to the pen, my daughter died of—well, they said it was poverty and the disgrace together. You've got a daughter, Judge, and I'm going to make you know how it feels to lose one. And I'm going to bite that district attorney that spoke against me. I'm free now, and I guess I've turned to rattlesnake all right. I feel like one. I don't say

202

much, but this is my rattle. Look out what I strike.

Yours respectfully,
RATTLESNAKE.

Judge Derwent threw the letter carelessly aside. It was nothing new to receive such epistles from desperate men whom he had been called upon to judge. He felt no alarm. Later on he showed the letter to Littlefield, the young district attorney, for Littlefield's name was included in the threat, and the judge was punctilious in matters between himself and his fellow men.

Littlefield honored the rattle of the writer, as far as it concerned himself, with a smile of contempt; but he frowned a little over the reference to the Judge's daughter, for he and Nancy Derwent were to be married in the fall.

Littlefield went to the clerk of the court and looked over the records with him. They decided that the letter might have been sent by Mexico Sam, a half-breed border desperado who has been imprisoned for manslaughter four years before. Then official duties crowded the matter from his mind, and the rattle of the revengeful serpent was forgotten.

203

Court was in session at Brownsville. Most of the cases to be tried were charges of smuggling, counterfeiting, post-office robberies, and violations of Federal laws along the border. One case was that of a young Mexican, Rafael Ortiz, who had been rounded up by a clever deputy marshal in the act of passing a counterfeit silver dollar. He had been suspected of many such deviations from rectitude, but this was the first time that anything provable had been fixed upon him. Ortiz languished cozily in jail, smoking brown cigarettes and waiting for trial. Kilpatrick, the deputy, brought the counterfeit dollar and handed it to the district attorney in his office in the court-house. The deputy and a reputable druggist were prepared to swear that Ortiz paid for a bottle of medicine with it. The coin was a poor counterfeit, soft, dull-looking, and made principally of lead. It was the day before the morning on which the docket would reach the case of Ortiz, and the district attorney was preparing himself for the trial.

"Not much need of having in high-priced experts to prove the coin's queer, is there, Kil?" smiled Littlefield, as he thumped the dollar down upon the table, where it fell with no more ring than would have come from a lump of putty.

"I guess the Greaser's as good as behind the

bars," said the deputy, easing up his holsters. "You've got him dead. If it had been just one time, these Mexicans can't tell good money from bad; but this little yaller rascal belongs to a gang of counterfeiters, I know. This is the first time I've been able to catch him doing the trick. He's got a girl down there in them Mexican jacals on the river bank. I seen her one day when I was watching him. She's as pretty as a red heifer in a flower bed."

Littlefield shoved the counterfeit dollar into his pocket, and slipped his memoranda of the case into an envelope. Just then a bright, winsome face, as frank and jolly as a boy's, appeared in the doorway, and in walked Nancy Derwent.

"Oh, Bob, didn't court adjourn at twelve to-day until to-morrow?" she asked of Littlefield.

"It did," said the district attorney, "and I'm very glad of it. I've got a lot of rulings to look up, and——"

"Now, that's just like you. I wonder you and Father don't turn to law books or rulings or something! I want you to take me out plover-shooting this afternoon. Long Prairie is just alive with them. Don't say no, please! I want to try my new twelve-bore hammerless. I've sent to the livery stable to engage Fly and Bess for the buckboard; they stand fire so nicely. I was sure you would go."

They were to be married in the fall. The glamour was at its height. The plovers won the day—or, rather, the afternoon—over the calf-bound authorities. Littlefield began to put his papers away.

There was a knock at the door. Kilpatrick answered it. A beautiful, dark-eyed girl with a skin tinged with the faintest lemon color walked into the room. A black shawl was thrown over her head and wound once around her neck.

She began to talk in Spanish, a voluble, mournful stream of melancholy music. Littlfield did not understand Spanish. The deputy did, and he translated her talk by portions, at intervals holding up his hands to check the flow of her words.

"She came to see you, Mr. Littlefield. Her name's Joya Treviñas. She wants to see you about—well, she's mixed up with that Rafael Ortiz. She's his— she's his girl. She says he's innocent. She says she made the money and got him to pass it. Don't you believe her, Mr. Littlefield. That's the way with these Mexican girls; they'll lie, steal, or kill for a fellow when they get stuck on him. Never trust a woman that's in love!"

"Mr. Kilpatrick!"

Nancy Derwent's indignant exclamation caused the deputy to flounder for a moment in attempting to explain that he had misquoted his own sentiments, and then he went on with the translation:

"She says she's willing to take his place in the jail if you'll let him out. She says she was down sick with the fever, and the doctor said she'd die if she didn't have medicine. That's why he passed the lead dollar on the drug store. She says it saved her life. This Rafael seems to be her honey, all right; there's a lot of stuff in her talk about love and such things that you don't want to hear."

It was an old story to the district attorney.

"Tell her," said he, "that I can do nothing. The case comes up in the morning, and he will have to make his fight before the court."

Nancy Derwent was not so hardened. She was looked with sympathetic interest at Joya Treviñas and at Littlefield alternately. The deputy repeated the district attorney's words to the girl. She spoke a sentence or two in a low voice, pulled her shawl closely about her face, and left the room.

"What did she say then?" asked the district attorney.

"Nothing special," said the deputy. "She said: 'If the life of the one'—let's see how it went—'*Si la vida de ella a quien tu amas*—if the life of the girl you love is ever in danger, remember Rafael Ortiz.'"

Kilpatrick strolled out through the corridor in the direction of the marshal's office.

"Can't you do anything for them, Bob?" asked Nancy. "It's such a little thing—just one counterfeit dollar—to ruin the happiness of two lives! She was in danger of death, and he did it to save her. Doesn't the law know the feeling of pity?"

"It hasn't a place in jurisprudence, Nan," said Littlefield, "especially *in re* the district attorney's duty. I'll promise you that the prosecution will not be vindictive; but the man is as good as convicted when the case is called. Witnesses will swear to his passing the bad dollar which I have in my pocket at this moment as 'Exhibit A.' There are no Mexicans on the jury, and it will vote Mr. Greaser guilty without leaving the box."

The plover-shooting was fine that afternoon, and in the excitement of the sport the case of Rafael and the grief of Joya Treviñas was forgotten. The district attorney and Nancy Derwent drove out from the town three miles along a smooth, grassy road, and then struck across a rolling prairie toward a heavy line of timber on Piedra Creek. Beyond this creek lay Long Prairie, the favorite haunt of the plover. As they were nearing the creek they heard the galloping of a horse to their right, and saw a man with black hair and a swarthy face riding toward the woods at a tangent, as if he had come up behind them.

"I've seen that fellow somewhere," said Littlefield, who had a memory for faces, "but I can't exactly place him. Some ranchman, I suppose, taking a short cut home."

They spent an hour on Long Prairie, shooting from the buckboard. Nancy Derwent, an active, outdoor Western girl, was pleased with her twelvebore. She had bagged within two brace of her companion's score.

They started homeward at a gentle trot. When within a hundred yards of Piedra Creek a man rode out of the timber directly toward them.

"It looks like the man we saw coming over," remarked Miss Derwent.

As the distance between them lessened, the district attorney suddenly pulled up his team sharply, with his eyes fixed upon the advancing horseman. That individual had drawn a Winchester from its scabbard on his saddle and thrown it over his arm.

"Now I know you, Mexico Sam!" muttered Littlefield to himself. "It *was* you who shook your rattles in that gentle epistle."

Mexico Sam did not leave things long in doubt. He had a nice eye in all matters relating to firearms, so when he was within good rifle range, but outside of danger from No. 8 shot, he threw up his Winchester and opened fire upon the occupants of the buckboard.

The first shot cracked the back of the seat within the two-inch space between the shoulders of Littlefield and Miss Derwent. The next went through the dashboard and Littlefield's trouser leg.

The district attorney hustled Nancy out of the buckboard to the ground. She was a little pale, but asked no questions. She had the frontier instinct that accepts conditions in an emergency without superfluous argument. They kept their guns in hand, and Littlefield hastily gathered some handfuls of cartridges from the pasteboard box on the seat and crowded them into his pockets.

"Keep behind the horses, Nancy," he commanded. "That fellow is a ruffian I sent to prison once. He's trying to get even. He knows our shot won't hurt him at that distance."

"All right, Bob," said Nancy, steadily. "I'm not afraid. But you come close, too. Whoa, Bess; stand still, now!"

She stroked Bess's mane. Littlefield stood with his gun ready, praying that the desperado would come within range.

But Mexico Sam was playing his vendetta along

safe lines. He was a bird of different feather from the plover. His accurate eye drew an imaginary line of circumference around the area of danger from bird-shot, and upon this line he rode. His horse wheeled to the right, and as his victims rounded to the safe side of their equine breastwork he sent a ball through the district attorney's hat. Once he miscalculated in making a detour, and overstepped his margin. Littlefield's gun flashed, and Mexico Sam ducked his head to the harmless patter of the shot. A few of them stung his horse, which pranced promptly back to the safety line.

The desperado fired again. A little cry came from Nancy Derwent. Littlefield whirled, with blazing eyes, and saw the blood trickling down her cheek.

"I'm not hurt, Bob—only a splinter struck me. I think he hit one of the wheel-spokes."

"Lord!" groaned Littlefield. "If I only had a charge of buckshot!"

The ruffian got his horse still, and took careful aim. Fly gave a snort and fell in the harness, struck in the neck. Bess, now disabused of the idea that plover were being fired at, broke her traces and galloped wildly away. Mexican Sam sent a ball neatly through the fullness of Nancy Derwent's shooting jacket.

"Lie down—lie down!" snapped Littlefield. "Close to the horse—flat on the ground—so." He almost threw her upon the grass against the back of the recumbent Fly. Oddly enough, at that moment the words of the Mexican girl returned to his mind:

"If the life of the girl you love is ever in danger, remember Rafael Ortiz."

Littlefield uttered an exclamation.

"Open fire on him, Nan, across the horse's back! Fire as fast as you can! You can't hurt him, but keep him dodging shot for one minute while I try to work a little scheme."

Nancy gave a quick glance at Littlefield, and saw him take out his pocket-knife and open it. Then she turned her face to obey orders, keeping up a rapid fire at the enemy.

Mexico Sam waited patiently until this inocuous fusillade ceased. He had plenty of time, and he did not care to risk the chance of a bird-shot in his eye if it could be avoided by a little caution. He pulled his heavy Stetson low down over his face until the shots ceased. Then he drew a little nearer, and fired with careful aim at what he could see of his victims above the fallen horse.

Neither of them moved. He urged his horse a

few steps nearer. He saw the district attorney rise
to one knee, and deliberately level his shotgun. He
pulled his hat down and awaited the harmless rattle of the tiny pellets.

The shotgun blazed with a heavy report. Mexico
Sam sighed, turned limp all over, and slowly fell
from his horse—a dead rattlesnake.

At ten o'clock the next morning court opened,
and the case of the United States *versus* Rafael
Ortiz was called. The district attorney, with his
arm in a sling, rose and addressed the court.

"May it please your honor," he said, "I desire
to enter a *nolle pros.* in this case. Even though the
defendant should be guilty, there is not sufficient
evidence in the hands of the government to secure
a conviction. The piece of counterfeit coin upon
the identity of which the case was built is not now
available as evidence. I ask, therefore, that the
case be stricken off."

At the noon recess, Kilpatrick strolled into the
district attorney's office.

"I've just been down to take a squint at old
Mexico Sam," said the deputy. "They've got him
laid out. Old Mexico was a tough outfit, I reckon.
The boys was wonderin' down there what you shot

him with. Some said it must have been nails. I never see a gun carry anything to make holes like he had."

"I shot him," said the district attorney, "with Exhibit A of your counterfeiting case. Lucky thing for me—and somebody else—that it was as bad money as it was! It sliced up into slugs very nicely. Say, Kil, can't you go down to the jacals and find where that Mexican girl lives? Miss Derwent wants to know."

A RAMBLE IN APHASIA

MY WIFE AND I parted on that morning in precisely our usual manner. She left her second cup of tea to follow me to the front door. There she plucked from my lapel the invisible strand of lint (the universal act of woman to proclaim ownership) and bade me take care of my cold. I had no cold. Next came her kiss of parting—the level kiss of domesticity flavored with Young Hyson. There was no fear of the extemporaneous, of variety spicing her infinite custom. With the deft touch of long malpractice, she dabbed awry my well-set scarf pin; and then, as I closed the door, I heard her morning slippers pattering back to her cooling tea.

When I set out I had no thought or premonition of what was to occur. The attack came suddenly.

For many weeks I had been toiling, almost night and day, at a famous railroad law case that I won triumphantly but a few days previously. In fact, I had been digging away at the law almost without cessation for many years. Once or twice good Doctor Volney, my friend and physician, had warned me.

"If you don't slacken up, Bellford," he said, "you'll go suddenly to pieces. Either your nerves or your brain will give way. Tell me, does a week pass in which you do not read in the papers of a case of aphasia—of some man lost, wandering nameless, with his past and his identity blotted out—and all from that little brain clot made by overwork or worry?"

"I always thought," said I, "that the clot in those instances was really to be found on the brains of the newspaper reporters."

Doctor Volney shook his head.

"The disease exists," he said. "You need a change or a rest. Court-room, office, and home—there is the only route you travel. For recreation you—read law books. Better take warning in time."

"On Thursday nights," I said, defensively, "my wife and I play cribbage. On Sundays she reads to me the weekly letter from her mother. That law books are not a recreation remains yet to be established."

216

That morning as I walked I was thinking of Doctor Volney's words. I was feeling as well as I usually did—possibly in better spirits than usual.

I woke with stiff and cramped muscles from having slept long on the incommodious seat of a day coach. I leaned my head against the seat and tried to think. After a long time I said to myself: "I must have a name of some sort." I searched my pockets. Not a card; not a letter; not a paper or monogram could I find. But I found in my coat pocket nearly $3,000 in bills of large denomination. "I must be some one, of course," I repeated to myself, and began to consider.

The car was well crowded with men, among whom, I told myself, there must have been some common interest, for they intermingled freely, and seemed in the best good humor and spirits. One of them—a stout, spectacled gentleman enveloped in a decided odor of cinnamon and aloes—took the vacant half of my seat with a friendly nod, and unfolded a newspaper. In the intervals between his periods of reading, we conversed, as travelers will, on current affairs. I found myself able to sustain the conversation on such subjects with credit, at least to my memory. By and by my companion said:

"You are one of us, of course. Fine lot of men the

217

West sends in this time. I'm glad they held the convention in New York; I've never been East before. My name's R. P. Bolder—Bolder & Son, of Hickory Grove, Missouri."

Though unprepared, I rose to the emergency, as men will when put to it.

Now must I hold a christening, and be at once babe, parson, and parent. My senses came to the rescue of my slower brain. The insistent odor of drugs from my companion supplied one idea: a glance at his newspaper, where my eye met a conspicuous advertisement, assisted me further.

"My name," said I, glibly, "is Edward Pinkhammer. I am a druggist, and my home is in Cornopolis, Kansas."

"I knew you were a druggist," said my fellow traveler, affably. "I saw the callous spot on your right forefinger where the handle of the pestle rubs. Of course, you are a delegate to our National Convention."

"Are all these men druggists?" I asked, wonderingly.

"They are. This car came through from the West. And they're your old-time druggists, too—none of your patent tablet-and-granule pharma-shootists that use slot machines instead of a prescription desk. We percolate our own paregoric and few garden seeds in the spring, and carrying a side roll our own pills, and we ain't above handling a line of confectionery and shoes. I tell you, Hampinker, I've got an idea to spring on this convention—new ideas is what they want. Now, you know the shelf bottles of tartar emetic and Rochelle salt Ant. et. Pot. Tart. and Sod. et. Pot. Tart.—one's poison, you know, and the other's harmless. It's easy to mistake one label for the other. Where do druggists mostly keep 'em? Why, as far apart as possible, on different shelves. That's wrong. I say keep 'em side by side, so when you want one you can always compare it with the other and avoid mistakes. Do you catch the idea?"

"All right! When I spring it on the convention you back it up. We'll make some of these Eastern orange-phosphate-and-massage-cream professors that think they're the only lozenges in the market look like hypodermic tablets."

"If I can be of any aid," I said, warming, "the two bottles of—er——"

"Tartrate of antimony and potash, and tartrate of soda and potash."

"Shall henceforth sit side by side," I concluded, firmly.

219

"Now, there's another thing," said Mr. Bolder. "For an excipient in manipulating a pill mass which do you prefer—the magnesia carbonate or the pulverized glycerrhiza radix?"

"The—er—magnesia," I said. It was easier to say than the other word.

Mr. Bolder glanced at me distrustfully through his spectacles.

"Give me the glycerrhiza," said he. "Magnesia cakes."

"Here's another one of these fake aphasia cases," he said, presently, handing me his newspaper, and laying his finger upon an article. "I don't believe in 'em. I put nine out of ten of 'em down as frauds. A man gets sick of his business and his folks and wants to have a good time. He skips out somewhere, and when they find him he pretends to have lost his memory—don't know his own name, and won't even recognize the strawberry mark on his wife's left shoulder. Aphasia! Tut! Why can't they stay at home and forget?"

I took the paper and read, after the pungent headlines, the following:

DENVER, June 12.—Elwyn C. Bellford, a prominent lawyer, is mysteriously missing from his home since three days ago, and all efforts to locate him have been in vain. Mr. Bellford is a well-known citizen of the highest standing, and has enjoyed a large and lucrative law practice. He is married and owns a fine home and the most extensive private library in the State. On the day of his disappearance, he drew quite a large sum of money from his bank. No one can be found who saw him after he left the bank. Mr. Bellford was a man of singularly quiet and domestic tastes, and seemed to find his happiness in his home and profession. If any clue at all exists to his strange disappearance, it may be found in the fact that for some months he has been deeply absorbed in an important law case in connection with the Q. Y. and Z. Railroad Company. It is feared that overwork may have affected his mind. Every effort is being made to discover the whereabouts of the missing man.

"It seems to me you are not altogether uncynical, Mr. Bolder," I said, after I had read the despatch. "This has the sound, to me, of a genuine case. Why should this man, prosperous, happily married, and respected, choose suddenly to abandon everything? I know that these lapses of memory do occur, and that men do find themselves adrift without a name, a history, or a home."

"Oh, gammon and jalap!" said Mr. Bolder. "It's

larks they're after. There's too much education nowadays. Men know about aphasia, and they use it for an excuse. The women are wise, too. When it's all over they look you in the eye, as scientific as you please, and say: 'He hypnotized me.'"

Thus Mr. Bolder diverted, but did not aid me with his comments and philosophy.

We arrived in New York about ten at night. I rode in a cab to a hotel, and I wrote my name "Edward Pinkhammer" in the register. As I did so I felt pervade me a splendid, wild, intoxicating buoyancy—a sense of unlimited freedom, of newly attained possibilities. I was just born into the world. The old fetters—whatever they had been—were stricken from my hands and feet. The future lay before me a clear road such as an infant enters, and I could set out upon it equipped with a man's learning and experience.

I thought the hotel clerk looked at me five seconds too long. I had no baggage.

"The Druggists' Convention," I said. "My trunk has somehow failed to arrive." I drew out a roll of money.

"Ah!" said he, showing an auriferous tooth, "we have quite a number of the Western delegates stopping here." He struck a bell for the boy.

I endeavored to give color to my rôle.

"There is an important movement on foot among us Westerners," I said, "in regard to a recommendation to the convention that the bottles containing the tartrate of antimony and potash, and the tartrate of sodium and potash be kept in a contiguous position on the shelf."

"Gentleman to three-fourteen," said the clerk, hastily. I was whisked away to my room.

The next day I bought a trunk and clothing, and began to live the life of Edward Pinkhammer. I did not tax my brain with endeavors to solve problems of the past.

It was a piquant and sparkling cup that the great island city held up to my lips. I drank of it gratefully. The keys of Manhattan belong to him who is able to bear them. You must be either the city's guest or its victim.

The following few days were as gold and silver. Edward Pinkhammer, yet counting back to his birth by hours only, knew the rare joy of having come upon so diverting a world full-fledged and unrestrained. I sat entranced on the magic carpets provided in theatres and roof-gardens, that transported one into strange and delightful lands full of frolicsome music, pretty girls, and grotesque, drolly extravagant parodies upon human kind. I went here and there at my own dear will, bound by no limits of space, time, or comportment. I dined in weird cabarets, at weirder *tables d'hôte* to the sound of Hungarian music and the wild shouts of mercurial artists and sculptors. Or, again, where the night life quivers in the electric glare like a kinetoscopic picture, and the millinery of the world, and its jewels, and the ones whom they adorn, and the men who make all three possible are met for good cheer and the spectacular effect. And among all these scenes that I have mentioned I learned one thing that I never knew before. And that is that the key to liberty is not in the hands of License, but Convention holds it. Comity has a toll-gate at which you must pay, or you may not enter the land of Freedom. In all the glitter, the seeming disorder, the parade, the abandon, I saw this law, unobtrusive, yet like iron, prevail. Therefore, in Manhattan you must obey these unwritten laws, and then you will be freest of the free. If you decline to be bound by them, you put on shackles.

Sometimes, as my mood urged me, I would seek the stately, softly murmuring palm rooms, redolent with high-born life and delicate restraint, in which to dine. Again I would go down to the waterways in steamers packed with vociferous, bedecked, un-checked love-making clerks and shop-girls to their crude pleasures on the island shores. And there was always Broadway—glistening, opulent, wily, vary-ing, desirable Broadway—growing upon one like an opium habit.

One afternoon as I entered my hotel a stout man with a big nose and a black mustache blocked my way in the corridor. When I would have passed around him, he greeted me with offensive famil-iarity.

"Hallo, Bellford!" he cried, loudly. "What the deuce are you doing in New York? Didn't know anything could drag you away from that old book den of yours. Is Mrs. B. along or is this a little busi-ness run alone, eh?"

"You have made a mistake, sir," I said, coldly, releasing my hand from his grasp. "My name is Pinkhammer. You will excuse me."

The man dropped to one side, apparently aston-ished. As I walked to the clerk's desk I heard him call to a bell boy and say something about tele-graph blanks.

"You will give me my bill," I said to the clerk, "and have my baggage brought down in half an hour. I do not care to remain where I am annoyed by confidence men."

I moved that afternoon to another hotel, a sedate, old-fashioned one on lower Fifth Avenue.

There was a restaurant a little way off Broadway where one could be served almost *al fresco* in a tropic array of screening flora. Quiet and luxury and a perfect service made it an ideal place in which to take luncheon or refreshment. One afternoon I was there picking my way to a table among the ferns when I felt my sleeve caught.

"Mr. Bellford!" exclaimed an amazingly sweet voice.

I turned quickly to see a lady seated alone—a lady of about thirty, with exceedingly handsome eyes, who looked at me as though I had been her very dear friend.

"You were about to pass me," she said, accusingly. "Don't tell me you did not know me. Why should we not shake hands—at least once in fifteen years?"

I shook hands with her at once. I took a chair opposite her at the table. I summoned with my eyebrows a hovering waiter. The lady was philandering with an orange ice. I ordered a *crème de menthe*. Her hair was reddish bronze. You could not look at it, because you could not look away from her eyes. But you were conscious of it as you are conscious of sunset while you look into the profundities of a wood at twilight.

"Are you sure you know me?" I asked.

"No," she said, smiling, "I was never sure of that."

"What would you think," I said, a little anxiously, "if I were to tell you that my name is Edward Pinkhammer from Cornopolis, Kansas?"

"What would I think?" she repeated with a merry glance. "Why, that you had not brought Mrs. Bellford to New York with you, of course. I do wish you had. I would have liked to see Marian." Her voice lowered slightly—"You haven't changed much, Elwyn."

I felt her wonderful eyes searching mine and my face more closely.

"Yes, you have," she amended, and there was a soft, exultant note in her latest tones; "I see it now. You haven't forgotten. You haven't forgotten for a year or a day or an hour. I told you you never could."

I poked my straw anxiously in the *crème de menthe*.

"I'm sure I beg your pardon," I said, a little un-

227

easy at her gaze. "But that is just the trouble. I have forgotten. I've forgotten everything."

She flouted my denial. She laughed deliciously at something she seemed to see in my face.

"I've heard of you at times," she went on. "You're quite a big lawyer out West—Denver, isn't it, or Los Angeles? Marian must be very proud of you. You knew, I suppose, that I married six months after you did. You may have seen it in the papers. The flowers alone cost two thousand dollars."

She had mentioned fifteen years. Fifteen years is a long time.

"Would it be too late," I asked, somewhat timorously, "to offer you congratulations?"

"Not if you dare do it," she answered, with such fine intrepidity that I was silent, and began to crease patterns on the cloth with my thumb nail.

"Tell me one thing," she said, leaning toward me rather eagerly—"a thing I have wanted to know for many years—just from a woman's curiosity, of course—have you ever dared since that night to touch, smell, or look at white roses—at white roses wet with rain and dew?"

I took a sip of *crème de menthe*.

"It would be useless, I suppose," I said, with a

sigh, "for me to repeat that I have no recollection at all about these things. My memory is completely at fault. I need not say how much I regret it."

The lady rested her arms upon the table, and again her eyes disdained my words and went traveling by their own route direct to my soul. She laughed softly, with a strange quality in the sound —it was a laugh of happiness—yes, and of content —and of misery. I tried to look away from her.

"You lie, Elwyn Bellford," she breathed, blissfully. "Oh, I know you lie!"

I gazed dully into the ferns.

"My name is Edward Pinkhammer," I said. "I came with the delegates to the Druggists' National Convention. There is a movement on foot for arranging a new position for the bottles of tartrate of antimony and tartrate of potash, in which, very likely, you would take little interest."

A shining landau stopped before the entrance. The lady rose. I took her hand, and bowed.

"I am deeply sorry," I said to her, "that I cannot remember. I could explain, but fear you would not understand. You will not concede Pinkhammer; and I really cannot at all conceive of the—the roses and other things."

"Good-bye, Mr. Bellford," she said, with her

happy, sorrowful smile, as she stepped into her carriage.

I attended the theatre that night. When I returned to my hotel, a quiet man in dark clothes, who seemed interested in rubbing his finger nails with a silk handkerchief, appeared, magically, at my side.

"Mr. Pinkhammer," he said, casually, giving the bulk of his attention to his forefinger, "may I request you step aside with me for a little conversation? There is a room here."

"Certainly," I answered.

He conducted me into a small, private parlor. A lady and a gentleman were there. The lady, I surmised, would have been unusually good-looking had her features not been clouded by an expression of keen worry and fatigue. She was of a style of figure and possessed coloring and features that were agreeable to my fancy. She was in a traveling dress; she fixed upon me an earnest look of extreme anxiety, and pressed an unsteady hand to her bosom. I think she would have started forward, but the gentleman arrested her movement with an authoritative motion of his hand. He then came, himself, to meet me. He was a man of forty, a little gray about the temples, and with a strong, thoughtful face.

"Bellford, old man," he said, cordially, "I'm glad to see you again. Of course we know everything is all right. I warned you, you know, that you were overdoing it. Now, you'll go back with us, and be yourself again in no time."

I smiled ironically.

"I have been 'Bellforded' so often," I said, "that it has lost its edge. Still, in the end, it may grow wearisome. Would you be willing at all to entertain the hypothesis that my name is Edward Pinkhammer, and that I never saw you before in my life?"

Before the man could reply a wailing cry came from the woman. She sprang past his detaining arms. "Elwyn!" she sobbed, and cast herself upon me, and clung tight. "Elwyn," she cried again, "don't break my heart. I am your wife—call my name once—just once. I could see you dead rather than this way."

I unwound her arms respectfully, but firmly.

"Madame," I said, severely, "pardon me if I suggest that you accept a resemblance too precipitately. It is a pity." I went on, with an amused laugh, as the thought occurred to me, "that this Bellford and I could not be kept side by side upon the same shelf like tartrates of sodium and antimony for purposes of identification. In order to understand this allusion," I concluded airily, "it may be necessary for you to keep an eye on the proceedings of the Druggists' National Convention.''

The lady turned to her companion, and grasped his arm.

"What is it, Doctor Volney? Oh, what is it?" she moaned.

He led her to the door.

"Go to your room for a while," I heard him say. "I will remain and talk with him. His mind? No, I think not—only a portion of the brain. Yes, I am sure he will recover. Go to your room and leave me with him."

The lady disappeared. The man in dark clothes also went outside, still manicuring himself in a thoughtful way. I think he waited in the hall.

"I would like to talk with you a while, Mr. Pinkhammer, if I may," said the gentleman who remained.

"Very well, if you care to," I replied, "and will excuse me if I take it comfortably; I am rather tired." I stretched myself upon a couch by a window and lit a cigar. He drew a chair near by.

"Let us speak to the point," he said, soothingly. "Your name is not Pinkhammer."

"I know that as well as you do," I said cooly. "But a man must have a name of some sort. I can

232

assure you that I do not extravagantly admire the name of Pinkhammer. But when one christens one's self suddenly, the fine names do not seem to suggest themselves. But, suppose it had been Schering-hausen or Scroggins! I think I did very well with Pinkhammer."

"Your name," said the other man, seriously, "is Elwyn C. Bellford. You are one of the first lawyers in Denver. You are suffering from an attack of asphasia, which has caused you to forget your identity. The cause of it was overapplication to your profession, and perhaps a life too bare of natural recreation and pleasures. The lady who has just left the room is your wife."

"She is what I would call a fine-looking woman," I said, after a judicial pause. "I particularly admire the shade of brown in her hair."

"She is a wife to be proud of. Since your disappearance, nearly two weeks ago, she has scarcely closed her eyes. We learned that you were in New York through a telegram sent by Isidore Newman, a traveling man from Denver. He said that he had met you in a hotel here, and that you did not recognize him."

"I think I remember the occasion," I said. "The fellow called me 'Bellford,' if I am not mistaken.

But don't you think it about time, now, for you to introduce yourself?"

"I am Robert Volney—Doctor Volney. I have been your close friend for twenty years, and your physician for fifteen. I came with Mrs. Bellford to trace you as soon as we got the telegram. Try, Elwyn, old man—try to remember!"

"What's the use to try?" I asked, with a little frown. "You say you are a physician. Is aphasia curable? When a man loses his memory does it return slowly, or suddenly?"

"Sometimes gradually and imperfectly; sometimes as suddenly as it went."

"Will you undertake the treatment of my case, Doctor Volney?" I asked.

"Old friend," said he, "I'll do everything in my power, and will have done everything that science can do to cure you."

"Very well," said I. "Then will you consider that I am your patient. Everything is in confidence now —professional confidence."

"Of course," said Doctor Volney.

I got up from the couch. Some one had set a vase of white roses on the centre table—a cluster of white roses, freshly sprinkled and fragrant. I threw them far out of the window, and then I laid myself upon the couch again.

"It will be best, Bobby," I said, "to have this cure happen suddenly. I'm rather tired of it all, anyway. You may go now and bring Marian in. But, oh, Doc," I said, with a sigh, as I kicked him on the shin—"good old Doc—it was glorious!"

THE POET AND THE
PEASANT

THE OTHER DAY a poet friend of mine, who has lived in close communion with nature all his life, wrote a poem and took it to an editor.

It was a living pastoral, full of the genuine breath of the fields, the song of birds, and the pleasant chatter of trickling streams.

When the poet called again to see about it, with hopes of a beefsteak dinner in his heart, it was handed back to him with the comment:

"Too artificial."

Several of us met over spaghetti and Duchess County chianti, and swallowed indignation with slippery forkfuls.

And there we dug a pit for the editor. With us was Conant, a well-arrived writer of fiction—a man who had trod on asphalt all his life, and who had never looked upon bucolic scenes except with sensations of disgust from the windows of express trains.

Conant wrote a poem and called it "The Doe and the Brook." It was a fine specimen of the kind of work you would expect from a poet who had strayed with Amaryllis only as far as the florist's windows, and whose sole ornithological discussion had been carried on with a waiter. Conant signed this poem, and we sent it to the same editor.

But this has very little to do with the story.

Just as the editor was reading the first line of the poem, on the next morning, a being stumbled off the West Shore ferryboat, and loped slowly up Forty-second Street.

The invader was a young man with light blue eyes, a hanging lip, and hair the exact color of the little orphan's (afterward discovered to be the earl's daughter) in one of Mr. Blaney's plays. His trousers were corduroy, his coat short-sleeved, with buttons in the middle of his back. One bootleg was outside the corduroys. You looked expectantly, in vain, at his straw hat for ear holes, its shape inaugurating the suspicion that it had been ravaged from a former equine possessor. In his hand was a valise—description of it is an impossible task; a

237

Boston man would not have carried his lunch and law books to his office in it. And above one ear, in his hair, was a wisp of hay—the rustic's letter of credit, his badge of innocence, the last clinging touch of the Garden of Eden lingering to shame the gold-brick men.

Knowingly, smilingly, the city crowds passed him by. They saw the raw stranger stand in the gutter and stretch his neck at the tall buildings. At this they ceased to smile, and even to look at him. It had been done so often. A few glanced at the antique valise to see what Coney "attraction" or brand of chewing gum he might be thus dinning into his memory. But for the most part he was ignored. Even the newsboys looked bored when he scampered like a circus clown out of the way of cabs and street cars.

At Eighth Avenue stood "Bunco Harry," with his dyed mustache and shiny, good-natured eyes. Harry was too good an artist not to be pained at the sight of an actor overdoing his part. He edged up to the countryman, who had stopped to open his mouth at a jewelry store window, and shook his head.

"Too thick, pal," he said, critically—"too thick by a couple of inches. I don't know what your lay is; but you've got the properties on too thick. That hay, now—why, they don't even allow that on Proctor's circuit any more."

"I don't understand you, mister," said the green one. "I'm not lookin' for any circus. I've just run down from Ulster County to look at the town, bein' that the hayin's over with. Gosh! but it's a whopper. I thought Poughkeepsie was some pumpkins; but this here town is five times as big."

"Oh, well," said "Bunco Harry," raising his eyebrows, "I didn't mean to butt in. You don't have to tell. I thought you ought to tone down a little, so I tried to put you wise. Wish you success at your graft, whatever it is. Come and have a drink, anyhow."

"I wouldn't mind having a glass of lager beer," acknowledged the other.

They went to a café frequented by men with smooth faces and shifty eyes, and sat at their drinks.

"I'm glad I come across you, mister," said Haylocks. "How'd you like to play a game or two of seven-up? I've got the keerds."

He fished them out of Noah's valise—a rare, inimitable deck, greasy with bacon suppers and grimy with the soil of cornfields.

"Bunco Harry," laughed loud and briefly.

"Not for me, sport," he said, firmly. "I don't go against that make-up of yours for a cent. But I still say you've overdone it. The Reubs haven't dressed like that since '79. I doubt if you could work Brooklyn for a key-winding watch with that layout."

"Oh, you needn't think I ain't got the money," boasted Haylocks. He drew forth a tightly rolled mass of bills as large as a teacup, and laid it on the table.

"Got that for my share of grandmother's farm," he announced. 'There's $950 in that roll. Thought I'd come to the city and look around for a likely business to go into."

"Bunco Harry" took up the roll of money and looked at it with almost respect in his smiling eyes.

"I've seen worse," he said, critically. "But you'll never do it in them clothes. You want to get light tan shoes and a black suit and a straw hat with a colored band, and talk a good deal about Pittsburg and freight differentials, and drink sherry for breakfast in order to work off phony stuff like that."

"What his line?" asked two or three shifty-eyed men of "Bunco Harry" after Haylocks had gathered up his impugned money and departed.

"The queer, I guess," said Harry. "Or else he's one of Jerome's men. Or some guy with a new graft. He's too much hayseed. Maybe that his—I

240

wonder now—oh, no, it couldn't have been real money."

Haylocks wandered on. Thirst probably asailed him again, for he dived into a dark groggery on a side street and bought beer. Several sinister fellows hung upon one end of the bar. At first sight of him their eyes brightened; but when his insistent and exaggerated rusticity became apparent their expressions changed to wary suspicion.

Haylocks swung his valise across the bar.

"Keep that a while for me, mister," he said, chewing at the end of a virulent claybank cigar.

"I'll be back after I knock around a spell. And keep your eye on it, for there's $950 inside of it, though maybe you wouldn't think so to look at me."

Somewhere outside a phonograph struck up a band piece, and Haylocks was off for it, his coat-tail buttons flopping in the middle of his back.

"Divvy, Mike," said the men hanging upon the bar, winking openly at one another.

"Honest, now," said the bartender, kicking the valise to one side. "You don't think I'd fall to that, do you? Anybody can see he ain't no jay. One of McAdoo's come-on squad, I guess. He's a shine if he made himself up. There ain't no parts of the country now where they dress like that since they run rural free delivery to Providence, Rhode Island.

241

If he's got nine-fifty in that valise it's a ninety-eight cent Waterbury that's stopped at ten minutes to ten."

When Haylocks had exhausted the resources of Mr. Edison to amuse he returned for his valise. And then down Broadway he gallivanted, culling the sights with his eager blue eyes. But still and evermore Broadway rejected him with curt glances and sardonic smiles. He was the oldest of the "gags" that the city must endure. He was so flagrantly impossible, so ultra rustic, so exaggerated beyond the most freakish products of the barnyards, the hayfield, and the vaudeville stage, that he excited only weariness and suspicion. And the wisp of hay in his hair was so genuine, so fresh and redolent of the meadows, so clamorously rural that even a shell-game man would have put up his peas and folded his table at the sight of it.

Haylocks seated himself upon a flight of stone steps and once more exhumed his roll of yellow-backs from the valise. The outer one, a twenty, he shucked off and beckoned to a newsboy.

"Son," said he, "run somewhere and get this changed for me. I'm mighty nigh out of chicken feed. I guess you'll get a nickel if you'll hurry up."

A hurt look appeared through the dirt on the newsy's face.

242

"Aw, watchert'ink! G'wan and get yer funny bill changed yerself. Dey ain't no farm clothes yer got on. G'wan wit yer stage money."

On a corner lounged a keen-eyed steerer for a gambling-house. He saw Haylocks, and his expression suddenly grew cold and virtuous.

"Mister," said the rural one. "I've heard of places in this here town where a fellow could have a good game of old sledge or peg a card at keno. I got $950 in this valise, and I come down from old Ulster to see the sights. Know where a fellow could get action on about $9 or $10? I'm goin' to have some sport, and then maybe I'll buy out a business of some kind."

The steerer looked pained, and investigated a white speck on his left forefinger nail.

"Cheese it, old man," he murmured, reproachfully. "The Central Office must be bughouse to send you out looking like such a gillie. You couldn't get within two blocks of a sidewalk crap game in them Tony Pastor props. The recent Mr. Scotty from Death Valley has got you beat a crosstown block in the way of Elizabethan scenery and mechanical accessories. Let it be skiddoo for yours. Nay, I know of no gilded halls where one may get a patrol wagon on the ace."

Rebuffed again by the great city that is so swift

to detect artificialities, Haylocks sat upon the curb and presented his thoughts to hold a conference.

"It's my clothes," said he; "durned if it ain't. They think I'm a hayseed and won't have nothin' to do with me. Nobody never made fun of this hat in Ulster County. I guess if you want folks to notice you in New York you must dress up like they do."

So Haylocks went shopping in the bazaars where men spake through their noses and rubbed their hands and ran the tape line ecstatically over the bulge in his inside pocket where reposed a red nubbin of corn with an even number of rows. And messengers bearing parcels and boxes streamed to his hotel on Broadway within the lights of Long Acre.

At 9 o'clock in the evening one descended to the sidewalk whom Ulster County would have foresworn. Bright tan were his shoes; his hat the latest block. His light gray trousers were deeply creased; a gay blue silk handkerchief flapped from the breast pocket of his elegant English walking coat. His collar might have graced a laundry window; his blond hair was trimmed close; the wisp of hay was gone.

For an instant he stood, resplendent, with the leisurely air of a boulevardier concocting in his mind the route for his evening pleasures. And then he turned down the gay, bright street with the easy and graceful tread of a millionaire.

But in the instant that he had paused the wisest and keenest eyes in the city had enveloped him in their field of vision. A stout man with gray eyes picked two of his friends with a lift of his eyebrows from the row of loungers in front of the hotel.

"The juicest jay I've seen in six months," said the man with gray eyes. "Come along."

It was half-past eleven when a man galloped into the West Forty-seventh Street Police Station with the story of his wrongs.

"Nine hundred and fifty dollars," he gasped, "all my share of grandmother's farm."

The desk sergeant wrung from him the name Jabez Bulltongue, of Locust Valley farm, Ulster County, and then began to take descriptions of the strong-arm gentlemen.

When Conant went to see the editor about the fate of his poem, he was received over the head of the office boy into the inner office that is decorated with the statuettes by Rodin and J. G. Brown.

"When I read the first line of 'The Doe and the Brook,'" said the editor, "I knew it to be the work of one whose life has been heart to heart with Nature. The finished art of the line did not blind me to that fact. To use a somewhat homely comparison, it was as if a wild, free child of the woods and fields were to don the garb of fashion and walk down Broadway. Beneath the apparel the man would show."

"Thanks," said Conant. "I suppose the check will be round on Thursday, as usual."

The morals of this story have somehow gotten mixed. You can take your choice of "Stay on the Farm" or "Don't Write Poetry."

THE ROBE OF PEACE

MYSTERIES follow one another so closely in a great city that the reading public and the friends of Johnny Bellchambers have ceased to marvel at his sudden and unexplained disappearance nearly a year ago. This particular mystery has now been cleared up, but the solution is so strange and incredible to the mind of the average man that only a select few who were in close touch with Bellchambers will give it full credence.

Johnny Bellchambers, as is well known, belonged to the intrinsically inner circle of the *élite*. Without any of the ostentation of the fashionable ones who endeavor to attract notice by eccentric display of wealth and show he still was *au fait* in everything that gave deserved lustre to his high position in the ranks of society.

Especially did he shine in the matter of dress. In

this he was the despair of imitators. Always correct, exquisitely groomed, and possessed of an unlimited wardrobe, he was conceded to be the best-dressed man in New York, and, therefore, in America. There was not a tailor in Gotham who would not have deemed it a precious boon to have been granted the privilege of making Bellchambers' clothes without a cent of pay. As he wore them, they would have been a priceless advertisement. Trousers were his especial passion. Here nothing but perfection would he notice. He would have worn a patch as quickly as he would have overlooked a wrinkle. He kept a man in his apartments always busy pressing his ample supply. His friends said that three hours was the limit of time that he would wear these garments without exchanging.

Bellchambers disappeared very suddenly. For three days his absence brought no alarm to his friends, and then they began to operate the usual methods of inquiry. All of them failed. He had left absolutely no trace behind. Then the search for a motive was instituted, but none was found. He had no enemies, he had no debts, there was no woman. There were several thousand dollars in his bank to his credit. He had never showed any tendency toward mental eccentricity; in fact, he was of a particularly calm and well-balanced temperament. Every means of tracing the vanished man made use of, but without avail. It was one of those cases—more numerous in late years—where men seem to have gone out like the flame of a candle, leaving not even a trail of smoke as a witness.

In May, Tom Eyres and Lancelot Gilliam, two of Bellchambers' old friends, went for a little run on the other side. While pottering around in Italy and Switzerland, they happened, one day, to hear of a monastery in the Swiss Alps that promised something outside of the ordinary tourist-beguiling attractions. The monastery was almost inaccessible to the average sight-seer, being on an extremely rugged and precipitous spur of the mountains. The attractions it possessed but did not advertise were, first, an exclusive and divine cordial made by the monks that was said to far surpass benedictine and chartreuse. Next a huge brass bell so purely and accurately cast that it had not ceased sounding since it was first rung three hundred years ago. Finally, it was asserted that no Englishman had ever set foot within its walls. Eyres and Gilliam decided that these three reports called for investigation.

It took them two days with the aid of two guides to reach the monastery of St. Gondrau. It stood upon a frozen, wind-swept crag with the snow piled about it in treacherous, drifting masses. They were hospitably received by the brothers whose duty it was to entertain the infrequent guest. They drank of the precious cordial, finding it rarely potent and reviving. They listened to the great, ever-echoing bell and learned that they were pioneer travelers, in those gray stone walls, over the Englishman whose restless feet have trodden nearly every corner of the earth.

At three o'clock on the afternoon they arrived, the two young Gothamites stood with good Brother Cristofer in the great, cold hallway of the monastery to watch the monks march past on their way to the refectory. They came slowly, pacing by twos, with their heads bowed, treading noiselessly with sandaled feet upon the rough stone flags. As the procession slowly filed past, Eyres suddenly gripped Gilliam by the arm. "Look," he whispered, eagerly, "at the one just opposite you now—the one on this side, with his hand at his waist—if that isn't Johnny Bellchambers then I never saw him!"

Gilliam saw and recognized the lost glass of fashion.

"What the deuce," said he, wonderingly, "is old Bell doing here? Tommy, it surely can't be he! Never heard of Bell having a turn for the religious. Fact is, I've heard him say things when a four-in-hand didn't seem to tie up just right that would bring him up for court-martial before any church."

"It's Bell, without a doubt," said Eyres, firmly, "or I'm pretty badly in need of an oculist. But think of Johnny Bellchambers, the Royal High Chancellor of swell togs and the Mahatma of pink teas, up here in cold storage doing penance in a snuff-colored bathrobe! I can't get it straight in my mind. Let's ask the jolly old boy that's doing the honors."

Brother Cristofer was appealed to for information. By that time the monks had passed into the refectory. He could not tell to which one they referred. Bellchambers? Ah, the brothers of St. Gondrau abandoned their worldly names when they took the vows. Did the gentlemen wish to speak with one of the brothers? If they would come to the refectory and indicate the one they wished to see, the reverend abbot in authority would, doubtless, permit it.

Eyres and Gilliam went into the dining hall and pointed out to Brother Cristofer the man they had seen. Yes, it was Johnny Bellchambers. They saw his face plainly now, as he sat among the dingy brothers, never looking up, eating broth from a coarse, brown bowl.

Permission to speak to one of the brothers was

granted to the two travelers by the abbot, and they waited in a reception room for him to come. When he did come, treading softly in his sandals, both Eyres and Gilliam looked at him in perplexity and astonishment. It was Johnny Bellchambers, but he had a different look. Upon his smooth-shaven face was an expression of ineffable peace, of rapturous attainment, of perfect and complete happiness. His form was proudly erect, his eyes shone with a serene and gracious light. He was as neat and well-groomed as in the old New York days, but how differently was he clad! Now he seemed clothed in but a single garment—a long robe of rough brown cloth, gathered by a cord at the waist, and falling in straight, loose folds nearly to his feet. He shook hands with his visitors with his old ease and grace of manner. If there was any embarrassment in that meeting it was not manifested by Johnny Bellchambers. The room had no seats; they stood to converse.

"Glad to see you, old man," said Eyres, somewhat awkwardly. "Wasn't expecting to find you up here. Not a bad idea, though, after all. Society's an awful sham. Must be a relief to shake the giddy whirl and retire to—er—contemplation and—er—prayer and hymns, and those things."

"Oh, cut that, Tommy," said Bellchambers,

cheerfully. "Don't be afraid that I'll pass around the plate. I go through these thing-um-bobs with the rest of these old boys because they are the rules. I'm Brother Ambrose here, you know. I've given just ten minutes to talk to you fellows. That's rather a new design in waistcoats you have on, isn't it, Gilliam? Are they wearing those things on Broadway now?"

"It's the same old Johnny," said Gilliam, joyfully. "What the devil—I mean why——— Oh, confound it! what did you do it for, old man?"

"Peel the bathrobe," pleaded Eyres, almost tearfully, "and go back with us. The old crowd'll go wild to see you. This isn't in your line, Bell. I know half a dozen girls that wore the willow on the quiet when you shook us in that unaccountable way. Hand in your resignation, or get a dispensation, or whatever you have to do to get a release from this ice factory. You'll get catarrh here, Johnny—and— My God! you haven't any socks on!"

Bellchambers looked down at his sandaled feet and smiled.

"You fellows don't understand," he said, soothingly. "It's nice of you to want me to go back, but the old life will never know me again. I have reached here the goal of all my ambitions. I am entirely happy and contented. Here I shall remain for the remainder of my days. You see this robe that I wear?" Bellchambers caressingly touched the straight-hanging garment: "At last I have found something that will not bag at the knees. I have attained——"

At that moment the deep boom of the great brass bell reverberated through the monastery. It must have been a summons to immediate devotions, for Brother Ambrose bowed his head, turned and left the chamber without another word. A slight wave of his hand as he passed through the stone doorway seemed to say a farewell to his old friends. They left the monastery without seeing him again.

And this is the story that Tommy Eyres and Lancelot Gilliam brought back with them from their latest European tour.

About the author of these

SHORT STORIES

William Sydney Porter, who signed his work with the *nom de plume* O. Henry, was born in Greensboro, N.C., on September 11, 1862, the son of a physician. As a young man he moved to Texas for his health, spending a couple of years on a ranch, then working in the land office and in an Austin bank. For a year he published and wrote most of a humorous weekly paper; he married, and joined the staff of the Houston Post. Then something still puzzling happened; he was accused of embezzling money from the Austin bank. Rather than face the charge, he fled to Central America. He learned that his wife was ill, and came back; after her death he served a short prison term. While there, he began to contribute short stories to the magazines; and soon after his release he settled in New York. His life was undramatic and he tended to be shy, except with the casual acquaintances of a park bench, but soon his ever-flowing stories were known around the world. He died on June 5, 1910. His stories have been collected in such volumes as THE FOUR MILLION, CABBAGES AND KINGS, and THE VOICE OF THE CITY.

LOOK FOR OUR MAGNUM CLASSICS